Magdalena Gottschalk:

Lindtzl Kingdom

M. Gail Grant

Copyright 2018 M. Gail Grant

Cover Designer: R.Atanassova@ElementiStudio

Keebie
Press
PO Box 5315
Canton, GA 30114

ISBN-13: 978-0-578-42135-3

~ Dedication ~

As I embark on this journey, I am constantly reminded and thankful for the blessings of my family, friends, and readers. I often think of all the childhood memories of my mother taking me to the local library to check out my next spooky mystery book. Sometimes the glimpses of yesterday flood through my soul as I sit at the computer writing away. My mother is in heaven but never forgotten. I am forever thankful that she introduced me to life within the pages of a book. I hope my readers experience the same excitement and intrigue as we discover Lindtzl Kingdom, together.

~ Author's Note ~

This book is a work of fiction. Names, characters, places, and events are all a product of the author's imagination or have been used in a fictitious nature. Any resemblance or link to actual people (living or deceased), places, or events, is coincidental in nature and does not represent the author's intent.

~ About the Author ~

Writing has always been my underlying passion in life. I hold a Bachelor of Science degree in Psychology and a formal minor in Sociology, as I felt understanding and studying human behavior on both the individual and collective levels would enhance anything and everything that I chose to do in life. Currently, I am a second-year graduate teaching assistant in the Master of Arts in Professional Writing program for English Composition at Kennesaw State University.

The desire to write has always been an integral part of who I am, and as my father's health began to decline, I decided it was time to seize the moment. Placing the rough-draft manuscript for book #1 of the ***Magdalena Gottschalk*** series in his hands was one of life's most precious moments. I attended a summer literary writer's camp around age twelve. Having cherished every moment of the experience, these childhood influences are found in MALB's many adventures.

I have always been an avid reader of books from intense young adult thrillers to light-hearted summer romances. During middle school summers, I used to stay up to the wee hours of the morning reading because I just couldn't put the book down.

This basic idea, not being able to put a book down, is the principal I have built upon while composing this middle-grade fantasy thriller series. It has moments of ease, moments of intensity, moments of spiritual exploration, and moments of humor, all the while encapsulating a paranormal and fantastical world. I have strived to collaboratively portray excitement and innocence of coming of age paradigms along with elements of faith woven through the underpinnings.

Hope, teamwork, friendship, and embracing differences are realistic components of life that MALB must face. There is a time for sweetness, a time for seriousness, and always a time for kindness and life lessons.

~M. Gail

Reader's Favorite 5 – Star Review:

"Grant's characters are marvelous! I loved seeing Gabriel and Magdalena act as a team and was quite intrigued to see how the ungainly Hubert comes into his own. The plot is exciting and fast-paced, and will thrill anyone who enjoys spells, trolls and daring rescues of queens in distress. Magdalena Gottschalk: Lindtzl Kingdom is most highly recommended."

~ J. Magnus, Reader's Favorite Reviewer

"If you're looking for a tale of magic and mystery, then this book is a great way to go…In Magdalena Gottschalk: Lindtzl Kingdom by M. Gail Grant, you're going to enjoy plenty of adventure and find out just what happens when friends come together to change the world."

~ S. DeWitt, Readers' Favorite Reviewer

"The fantasy system of the story is well imagined, with different 'demons' and an exciting variety of foes for the young heroes to face. Magdalena herself is, by and large, a normal girl thrown into extraordinary circumstances, and the Christian theme underlying the tale doesn't distract from the fantasy plot, but enhances it cohesively. Overall, Magdalena Gottschalk: Lindtzl Kingdom is a recommended read in a fun fantasy series, suitable for all."

~ K.C. Finn, Readers' Favorite Reviewer

~ Contents ~

ENCHANTED SPELLS
~ One ~

Christmas in Lily Brooke had been such a sentimental time for the children.

Magdalena and the rest of the gang had spent the week before the holiday, wondering if they would escape the kingdom of Lindtzl and make it back home in time for the celebration.

It seemed every time the six friends got together, an adventure would be waiting. And an adventure they had this last time, for sure.

Why what had begun as a reminiscent camping trip amongst dear childhood friends had turned deadly.

Who would have thought that MALB, The Mystical Alliance of Lily Brooke, would encounter such a hideous beast as a three-headed werewolf!

Of course, this wasn't to mention the treacherous ride down the slippery slope, the ominous and hidden vortex, or the booby-trapped castle they had happened upon in The Enchanted Forest.

Magdalena gave a slight shudder as the events of the last few weeks began to replay in her mind.

Everything had ended well, she thought.

But life-threatening adventures seemed to follow the six group of friends like hunting dogs tracking a fox's scent.

She couldn't help but stifle a sly grin. Even though there had been scenarios of quite desperate odds, she wouldn't trade the experiences with her closest friends for anything in the world.

The Mystical Alliance of Lily Brooke had been inseparable for years. Comprised of six thirteen-year-old children, the childhood club had been together since their Kindergarten days.

In the early beginnings, MALB's main purpose was to become the crime-solving crew of Lily Brooke. The group met each week in anticipation of someone having discovered a hot mystery just waiting to be solved.

After a few hours of fictional crime-solving, the friends always ended up playing a game of royals and robbers, which was nothing more than a glorified game of hide-and-go-seek.

The best part of the day was when everyone seemed to forget if they were a royal or a robber, and all chaos ensued.

Ah, those were the days, thought Magdalena.

Taking a deep breath, she closed her eyes to focus while attempting to channel her inner thoughts. This was turning out to be much harder than she had hoped.

With the unexpected adventures that always seemed to find her, Magdalena decided it was time to learn more about her newly discovered skill, black magic.

Specifically, she wanted to add a few tools in her tool belt. Yes, it was time she began learning those ancient and secretive enchanted spells that would help protect her friends and community from any forces of evil that decided to rear their ugly heads. And based upon previous experience, some of the evil hiding in the shadows had seriously very ugly heads.

"Levante!" shouted Magdalena.

She opened her eyes to see if the spell had worked.

Disappointed, she sat down on the tree stump beside her while pondering what she was doing wrong.

She picked up the little black book again and began to re-read the print before her eyes.

"Hi, Mags! Whatcha doing?" asked Gabriel.

Magdalena was so startled she fell off the tree stump and landed flat on her back.

She thought for sure that here, underneath the old oak tree, no one would find her.

How in the world did Gabriel know where to look for me? She wondered.

"Gabriel, how did you know where to find me?" stammered Magdalena.

Gabriel couldn't help but give a little giggle as he looked down at his best friend lying on her back.

She looked something between stunned and embarrassed, he surmised.

He held out his hand to help his favorite girl back up off the cold ground.

"Well, Mags, it wasn't too difficult. We have been meeting at this old tire swing and oak tree for about seven years now," he proudly stated. "If you aren't at home, and yes, I stopped by, and your mom said you were out taking a walk, then I know to try here first. Looks like I have interrupted something?"

"I'm just glad it was you that found me and not someone else," smiled Magdalena as she stood to her feet with Gabriel's help.

"What were you working on so intensely?" inquired Gabriel.

"Do you see this book, Gabriel?"

Magdalena held up the little black book that she had been reading when Gabriel decided to scare the bejeezus out of her.

"Haven't seen it before, I don't think," said Gabriel as he looked slightly confused as to where this conversation was going.

"I had forgotten all about it to be honest with you. Do you remember the night late last fall when we met at Saint Irmgardis and crawled inside of that elevator shaft to eavesdrop on the private town hall meeting?" asked Magdalena.

"Do I remember? Are you serious? Worst night of our lives, Mags. I'm fairly certain none of MALB has forgotten that night," replied Gabriel.

Had his precious Mags completely lost her mind?

Magdalena gave a little sigh, as she was so preoccupied with what she had to say next that she had forgotten what a night it had truly been.

"Oh, yes, yes, yes, sorry. No kidding. I didn't mean to lessen the severity of the night, as it was

5

quite frightening. I was just focused on what I have to tell you," responded Magdalena excitedly.

"That night before we met when I was heading to bed, I happened to see my parents at the kitchen table. They were leaning over something and whispering. I tried to spy but couldn't hear their conversation. So, I popped my head around the corner and said good night."

"Mags, where is this going?" asked Gabriel.

Usually, Magdalena got straight to the point, but she seemed almost to be walking herself through the events instead of informing him of what she was really talking about.

"Oh, sorry, Gabriel. As I popped my head around the corner, my mother slid a little black book into her lap under the table. I knew then my mom and dad were discussing something they didn't want to share with me."

"Did you ever figure out what it was?" asked Gabriel.

"Yes! That is where I am going with this. Here, check this out!" exclaimed Magdalena.

Gabriel looked down to see Magdalena holding a thin, solid black book in her hand. It didn't appear to be anything special, no writing on the front of it, so he wondered why she was so intrigued.

"Well, Mags, it just looks like a little black book to me," suggested Gabriel.

"And that is probably what it is meant to look like!" shouted Magdalena. "But it is much, much, more than that. This right here in my hand is a book on enchanted spells!"

Gabriel felt his bottom jaw drop. Where had Magdalena found a book on spells?

Magdalena could see the look of disbelief on Gabriel's face, and it was exactly what she had been expecting.

She knew this was going to surprise him, which was something not easy to do. Gabriel was as sharp as a tack and not someone that could be fooled very easily.

"So, Mags, where did you find that book? And better yet, what are you doing here in the woods by the tire swing all alone with that book?"

Gabriel knew something was up. It had only been a few weeks since the last adventure, and he wasn't sure he was quite ready for any more surprises.

"I was helping my mother in her boutique the other day, you know, Leona's Dream Catchers?"

Magdalena didn't give Gabriel a chance to respond before she pushed on with her story.

"In the back room where my mother prepares the incense, herbs, and dries the lily root, she has a shelf labeled with various things. Underneath one of the jars labeled 'twisted shrooms' was this little book. I instantly knew it was the same book I had seen that night. It has always weighed on my mind, as I was very curious as to what my parents were hiding. But there was no way to figure it out. That is until I saw this book on the shelf in my mother's back storeroom!"

Gabriel wasn't quite sure he shared Magdalena's excitement.

Leona Gottschalk was a kind-hearted and devoted member of the Lily Brooke community. Her boutique, Leona's Dream Catchers, supplied their small town with incense, dried herbs, crystals of all sorts, and the most beautiful dream catchers one had ever seen.

But, she was a witch.

And when it came to witches and wizards having secret conversations and little black hidden books, well Gabriel just didn't think it fell into the category of spectacular news.

"Mags, do I want to know what that black book has in store for me? Is this going to throw us into the next adventure? We just survived the last one!" he exclaimed.

"Oh, Gabriel, no! Don't worry! I won't drag you into a battle with the enchanted demons of Lily Brooke's past again. They are locked up forever; you know that. And, their awful three-headed werewolf gatekeeper has been beaten. Little Skully is the best pet anyone could ever have. Well, since we defeated the demonic spell and the three-headed werewolf reverted to a little dog. You know come to think of it, that was fairly intense, Gabriel," whispered Magdalena.

"Uh, yes, it was, Mags. Don't worry, I haven't forgotten about flying down the slippery slope and the treacherous winter terrain, or sliding into the puddle through the hidden vortex, or traipsing through The Enchanted Forest only to get to the castle and then finding out it was booby-trapped with this demonic, crazy, three-headed werewolf trying to kill us. Or, being thrown around by a wicked enchanted tree root and surviving a long fall to the bottom of a deserted damp well. Magdalena, being friends with you does not leave one bored," laughed Gabriel.

Gee, hearing all the adventures from a few weeks ago, almost made Magdalena tired.

"Gabriel, please don't forget the best part," giggled Magdalena.

"Oh, I won't forget anything about that excursion," grinned Gabriel. "Especially the part where we fed the hungry werewolf and beat the demonic curse. And yes, Skully, as you named him, will be a wonderful pet for Queen Lindtzl."

"I miss her, Gabriel. She seemed so lonely, and it was very kind of her to give us that snow globe just so we could return and visit her at any time," remembered Magdalena.

Gabriel could sense what was coming, and he was certain the rest of MALB would not be ready to return to Lindtzl Kingdom and The Enchanted Forest any time soon.

Although MALB was very thankful to the queen for sending them home in time for the holidays, he didn't think their appreciativeness would outweigh the forces of evil that had taken over the queen's land.

Lindtzl Kingdom had once been a beautiful enchanted forest where witches, wizards, demons, werewolves, and other enchanted beings had lived harmoniously. But everything took a turn for the worse when the demon head had fallen in love with Magdalena's mother, Leona. She had rejected his love as Paulos Gottschalk was the man of her dreams.

The grand demon had unleashed wrath so vicious and widespread that it not only affected the citizens of Lily Brooke but had upset the homeostasis conditions found throughout Lindtzl Kingdom.

"Gabriel are you there?" asked Magdalena. "You look like you are in a trance. Is everything okay?"

"Oh, sorry, Mags. I was just thinking about the queen and everything she had been through when the demons had roamed the kingdom. I'm so glad they are now locked up inside of the hidden lanterns," responded Gabriel.

"Yes, the queen seemed very happy when we defeated the curse, which allowed her to go back home to her cherished castle. I know living in the winter wonderland must have been amazing, but now she is back home in Lindtzl Castle, where she spent her last happy days with her king before he was killed," surmised Magdalena.

"So, what does that black book you are holding have to do with Lindtzl Kingdom, or what you were focused on when I startled you?" inquired Gabriel.

"Right! Well, like I was saying, I found this book underneath a jar labeled 'twisted shrooms,'" replied Magdalena. "This book, Gabriel, is an ancient book of secret spells."

"Oh, boy," was all Gabriel could muster.

He knew in the pit of his stomach this was going to go from bad to worse and real fast.

Magdalena laughed, quite excited at the prospect of impressing Gabriel further.

"Watch this; I was trying to perfect this spell when you walked up and scared me," Magdalena exclaimed with a little pout of the lips.

Gabriel watched as Magdalena closed her eyes and entered her infamous trance-like state.

He wasn't sure what was going to happen from here, so he decided to take a few small steps backward just in case something went a little hairy.

With a look of determination on her face and her eyes closed, Magdalena was now in full witch mode.

Gabriel didn't utter a word or move a muscle. There was no way he wanted to come between a witch and her spell. With his luck, he would accidentally turn into some creepy frog or something worse.

Holding his breath, he watched Magdalena in suspense.

Gabriel wasn't sure if it was his imagination, but the air seemed to become a little cooler. He wasn't one hundred percent sure because it was already a dreary and overcast mid-January day, but something about the ambiance surrounding him seemed to change slightly.

Before Gabriel had another thought, Magdalena opened her eyes and pointed her finger at a large rock lying about three feet in front of her.

"Levante!" she shouted with such conviction that Gabriel jumped in his own tracks.

Right before their very eyes, the large rock began to rise in the air and float before them. It just stayed there suspended in the air at eye level, as though it were simply frozen in time.

Magdalena didn't break eye contact with the rock. Her hands were outstretched in front of her, palms out, and fingers spread.

Gabriel realized she was controlling the rock with her gaze.

Pleased with the results, Magdalena began to slowly lower her arms, and the large, floating rock did the same.

Within a few moments, the rock was again resting peacefully where it had laid when Gabriel had arrived.

Magdalena looked at Gabriel and said, "I did it, Gabriel! I made the rock float in the air, and I was able to control its movement with my gaze. Did you see it?"

Gabriel had no response other than the complete conversation in his head, with no one other than himself. It volleyed between panic, to excitement, back to panic, to pure fear.

One thing was for sure, Magdalena never seemed to disappoint.

Knowing Gabriel was at a loss for words, Magdalena gave a slight cackle and said, "Ready for more?"

TWISTED SHROOMS
~ Two ~

Realizing that Magdalena must have been busy these last few weeks working on her enchanted talents, Gabriel wondered what her plan entailed.

The adventures they happened upon from following the crooked trail had left her feeling depressed and remorseful.

With nothing but a newfound sense of adventure, the group had decided to traipse through the dense woods following the mysterious crooked path.

As it wove deeper into the thickest part of the wooded area, it stopped short right in front of what turned out to be a sacrificial cave.

Determined to get to the bottom of their mystery, the group had pushed on through the cave to discover a hidden treehouse.

Somehow, all of these adventures led from one mysterious circumstance to another, and well, through it all, Magdalena had discovered her life purpose.

She was a witch.

Her mother was a witch.

They had even discovered that Hubert's parents, Gerard and Betsy Mueller, were both a witch and a wizard.

My, my, how life had changed a few months ago. But all this discovery had thrown Magdalena into quite the tailspin.

Missing his friends, Gabriel had begged Magdalena to get the gang back together and go camping. She had reluctantly agreed, although feeling a little apprehensive about meeting at the old oak tree again.

The previous experience at that tree hadn't been all that great, well, when they had discovered the death threat carved into the tree.

Nonetheless, Magdalena had joined her friends, and everyone had been so excited that night to once again be back in each other's company.

Then there was the whole werewolf in the night issue, which led to the slippery slope adventure.

Getting back home right before Christmas had been quite the relief.

At the end of their last adventure, Gabriel thought he had sensed a resolve within Magdalena of being completely done with all this witch stuff.

Yet, here she was practicing spells alone by the tire swing hanging from the old oak tree. It was a stark contrast to her demeanor a few weeks prior.

Girls, they seemed to be quite difficult to figure out, thought Gabriel.

"Hey Mags, why do I get this unsettled feeling that you have something up your sleeve?" inquired Gabriel.

He figured it was much better to get this situation aired out now before Magdalena spent any time planning his future. He was completely, totally, and one hundred percent done with demons. And, he meant it — no more excursions for him.

"Now Gabriel, you know I always have something up my sleeve. And of course, it will be much worse now since I am learning how to cast spells. Pretty soon, you will be able to ask me what spells I have up my sleeve," laughed Magdalena.

Gabriel sure loved his precious Mags, but he wasn't quite sure he shared in her sense of humor.

He liked the old Mags, the one that didn't play with black magic. She was always up for a challenge or adventure, and he actually had liked that about her.

But now that she was a witch, he wished she could tailor the adventurous side, just a touch.

"That's what I am afraid of," replied Gabriel.

He could feel the sense of dread climbing from the pit of his stomach to the back of his throat.

"I can't believe you are able to make a stone float in the air just by your gaze, Mags. That is so cool."

Regardless of his apprehension, he was glad for his best friend. Her excitement and intrigue showed on her face, and he wanted her to be happy beyond anything else.

"Thanks! I have lots more to learn, but the way I figure it, if I have all of this new ability, then I should learn how to use it as much as I can. We never know when the demons will surprise us again, or what may lie ahead for all of Lily Brooke," replied Magdalena.

Magdalena's words were true, Gabriel knew. He didn't necessarily want to agree with her, but she had a good point.

"Well, Mags, as far as I am concerned, I hope never to see any of those demons ever again. Let's hope you never need your black magic skills," grumbled Gabriel.

"I agree. But as we learned in the last two adventures, it is always better to be safe than sorry," stated Magdalena, as a matter of fact as she could muster.

"What other spells can you do?"

"This is as far as I have gotten. I have a feeling, things will come easier now that I have learned the art of concentration," replied Magdalena.

"What do you mean, Mags?"

"Well, the first spell in this book is Levante. It teaches a witch or wizard to channel all of their inner energy into one spot, one object. Using the energy in your brain, you simply concentrate on whatever object you are focused on and create your own reality."

"Uh, I don't get it, Mags," said Gabriel as he stood there with his hands tucked into his pockets, shuffling his feet.

"Let me explain. You create your own reality. In other words, you pretend to see what you want to see, and the result becomes what your mind is telling your body and soul is happening. For example, I want to see the rock floating in the air in front of me. So, I concentrate all of my energy looking at the rock and kind of willing it to levitate in the air. With all of the intense energy focused on the rock, my reality creates the levitating rock," said Magdalena.

Gabriel stood there looking at Magdalena while trying to make sense of her words.

"I get it now! What a cool spell to know," said Gabriel.

"Yes, I have a feeling there will be a good bit of information found in this little black book," grinned Magdalena.

As Gabriel stood there watching his friend practice the new spell over and over, he noticed almost a twinkling in her eyes. Although the news of being a witch had been difficult for Magdalena, in true Magdalena fashion, she seemed to now be adapting quite nicely and embracing the intrigue instead of licking her wounds.

"Won't your mom miss the book?" asked Gabriel.

As exciting as all of this was, he would hate to see what happened if Leona discovered the book missing. They barely escaped the tainted flu vaccine a few months ago that had been tampered with black magic.

The vaccine was a truth serum, and memory cocktail added to the seasonal flu shot, aimed at finding out what secrets the community may be withholding about the demons in Lily Brooke's past.

The last thing Gabriel wanted was another close call like the last one.

Hmm, thought Magdalena. *Gabriel may have a good point.*

"You know, you may have a really good point. I don't ever want to enter a vaccine recovery room again and have to suffer through the inquisitive eyes of my mother. Witch or no witch, she is still my mother," surmised Magdalena.

"How about we head back to your mom's store and hide that little book before she makes the discovery?" suggested Gabriel.

"Works for me," responded Magdalena.

The two friends grabbed hands and began walking towards Leona's Dream Catchers.

Gabriel was quite anxious to get that little black book back to where it belonged. The snow crunched underneath their feet as they left the old oak tree in the distance.

"I sure hope your mom is still at home and didn't decide to go in to work this afternoon," said Gabriel.

Magdalena wasn't quite sure why Gabriel seemed to be so tense this afternoon. At first, she had kind of laughed it off, but now it had her a little perplexed.

"Gabriel, is everything okay at home? Is your dad doing okay?" inquired Magdalena.

She adored Mr. Bach. He was such a kind man and very talented, too. He supplied most of Lily Brooke with beautiful hand-crafted wrought iron gates.

"He is doing great. He had one of his best holiday seasons yet with sales. I miss spending time with him, but his business is soaring, which makes him so happy. Why do you ask?"

"You seem to be a little on edge today, and I was just wondering if something is going on," replied Magdalena.

Gabriel had several thoughts running through his head, and he wasn't sure how much he wanted to share with Magdalena.

He had always been completely open and truthful with her, but as they were getting older, he was experiencing new feelings and thoughts that he wasn't sure he was ready to share.

Magdalena noticed Gabriel seemed lost in thought, but she didn't want to pry. She just wanted to make sure her favorite person on earth was doing okay.

"Oh, it's nothing, Mags. I didn't sleep very well last night. Nothing to worry about, I promise," whispered Gabriel.

He didn't look her in the eye, as he knew Magdalena well enough to know she would for sure know he was lying. And, who knows what extra intuition she may now possess being a witch and all.

Magdalena dropped the topic as they continued to head towards Leona's boutique. She wasn't sure she believed Gabriel's response, but she knew if he didn't share what was bothering him with her, he probably wouldn't share it with anyone. As determined as she always was, even she knew sometimes it was better just to let it go.

Within a few minutes, Gabriel and Magdalena found themselves at the boutique. They walked around to the back of the store, and Magdalena pulled out a key.

"Ah! I see you have a key now, Mags. That sure makes sneaking in here much easier," laughed Gabriel.

He was trying to lighten the mood a little since Magdalena had sensed his uneasiness.

"Yes. I am working for my mother now a few hours a week, just helping out in the store. Anyway, now I have a key," stated Magdalena.

A few seconds later, the friends were inside the boutique.

Magdalena led Gabriel to the back storeroom, where all of the supplies were kept.

Sure enough, there was a tall wooden shelf with mason jar after mason jar full of spices, herbs, powders, and all kinds of mysterious-looking specimens.

Gabriel couldn't help the shutter than coursed through his veins.

Magdalena didn't seem to notice.

"Here it is, the jar labeled 'twisted shrooms' exactly where I found it," said Magdalena.

Magdalena lifted the jar and placed the little black book where it belonged. She was hoping this would make Gabriel feel a little better. She hated it when he seemed to be distant.

"Good!" replied Gabriel. "Now, let's get out of here. I get the creeps in this place."

Magdalena laughed, "What is wrong with you, silly?"

"Mags, didn't you wonder what a twisted shroom was?" asked Gabriel.

Magdalena looked as though a light bulb illuminated inside of her head.

Uh oh, thought Gabriel. *What did I do? I should have been quiet!*

"You have a good point, Gabriel. I got so excited when I found the book that I didn't put much thought into the jar," murmured Magdalena.

Before Gabriel could respond or even have another thought, Magdalena lifted the mason jar above her head and began turning it in the light.

Her thoughts were going a million miles a minute. She had never heard her mother mention twisted shrooms and didn't recall ever seeing or hearing of them before.

Curiosity was now in over-drive. She HAD to find out what a twisted shroom was, and why in the world her mother would have them in the stockroom.

Gabriel could almost see his life flash in front of his very eyes as Magdalena picked the little black book back up off the shelf.

She flipped to the index in the back and must have found something as the smile that lit up her face was bold and beautiful.

Magdalena looked at Gabriel and said, "There is a spell called twisted shrooms! We HAVE to see what it is used for; we just have to!"

The pleading in Magdalena's eyes was enough for Gabriel to swallow the huge lump that had formed in his throat.

This is what I get for opening my mouth, he thought.

Gabriel sighed and said, "Somehow, Mags, I knew you were going to say that."

Magdalena sat down on the floor in her mother's storeroom, cross-legged.

After a moment of contemplation, she opened the black book to chapter three labeled 'Twisted Shrooms.'

What could be so bad? She thought.

WITCHY SOUP
~ Three ~

Gabriel sat down on the floor beside Magdalena and was fairly certain the pounding hammer inside of his head was his own heartbeat.

He glanced down at the words that seemed to jump from the page of the little book. His eye caught the familiar term 'lily root' quickly.

"Magdalena, tell me we don't have another lily root spell," quivered Gabriel as he tried to cover up his nervousness.

Although lily root had saved his life on various occasions, he knew without a doubt that anything involving lily root would also involve demons or other dark forces of some sort.

Heck, at this point, Gabriel was slowly beginning to realize that any spell in that book would somehow involve demons or other dark forces.

Gabriel missed the simple days. He missed the naïveness of yesterday when the only troubles he had was figuring out how to balance homework, spending time with his friends, and helping his dad in the blacksmith shop.

Now, it seemed Gabriel was constantly looking over his shoulder. Once you had the experience of battling a demon face to face, somehow, it never seemed to leave you permanently.

Realizing that Mags had been quietly reading for a while and had left his questions unanswered, he begrudgingly snapped back to reality.

"What? What is it, Mags? Cat got your tongue?" asked Gabriel.

Magdalena had been lost in deep thought. Her mind was already in Hubert's barn as she now knew what needed to happen next.

"Sorry, Gabriel. I was just thinking about getting to Hubert's barn as fast as we can," she replied.

"Wait, what?" asked Gabriel. "Why are we going to Hubert's barn?"

"Because we need to make witchy soup," said Magdalena. "Hurry, let's go!"

Before Gabriel could respond, Magdalena stood up and grabbed him by the hand. Before he knew it, he was on his feet and trotting for the back door.

Within a few moments, the pair had turned off the lights in the boutique and locked the back door.

As Magdalena and Gabriel exited the back of the building, the sun was dipping lower on the horizon. Winter in Lily Brooke had the sun setting by five o'clock in the evening. The days were short, and the air was brisk.

Gabriel knew better than to disturb Magdalena's thoughts as they quickly headed towards Hubert's home on Wildwood Lane. She hadn't answered his questions yet, which meant her mind was several stages beyond the current moment in time.

The pair had been friends long enough for Gabriel to not only understand her quirks but long enough for him to know her thoughts before she even spoke.

As they turned down the long gravel road leading to Hubert's house, Magdalena couldn't help but give a slight shiver. Something about the façade of the home had never sat well with her soul. It was such a stark contrast to the rest of the homes found in Lily Brooke.

Hubert's home featured a blending of stone and rod iron. It had always reminded Magdalena of what a castle hiding in plain sight would look like. The tall steeples seemed to beckon a mysterious vibe, and she had never figured out why her instincts would always remind her to remain on guard. There was always this sense of uneasiness radiating from the Mueller home.

But, Magdalena had learned the hard way to always pay attention to her sixth sense. It had steered her well right up to this point in her life, and she knew when she crossed over the front door threshold, the detective in her would stand tall.

Magdalena adored Gerard and Betsy Mueller, Hubert's parents. Although recent discovery had revealed that Gerard and Betsy were a wizard and a witch, respectively, they were a pinnacle sight in the town of Lily Brooke.

Gerard grew most of the food that supplied the small town. He would be out tilling the land from morning till dusk.

Betsy was a caregiver for the sick residents of Lily Brooke. She would travel from home to home, tending to the elderly and severely ill. She had a warmth about her that seemed to comfort her patients.

Magdalena was ringing the doorbell, and Gabriel was standing there, dreading what may happen next. He knew all too well that Magdalena was typically full of surprises.

The Mueller door swung open, and Hubert stood there looking like he had just awoken from a deep sleep. His short blonde hair stood spikey on top of his head, smashed into a weird-looking cowlick on the crown of his head.

Magdalena and Gabriel stood there eyeing Hubert from head to toe as it wasn't often he seemed to be caught completely off guard.

"Oh, hi guys. Didn't expect you here today," stammered Hubert as he realized he probably looked a fright.

Feeling slightly embarrassed, he motioned for his two friends to come on inside the house.

Magdalena didn't want to step over the threshold but knew it would appear rude if she didn't.

As Hubert closed the front door behind them, he turned to his two best friends and asked, "What's up, guys?"

Magdalena looked at Gabriel and then back at Hubert.

"Can we go see Sugar Baby?" she asked.

Hubert got this strange expression on his face as he wondered why in the world Magdalena and Gabriel would want to see his horse on a late Sunday afternoon in mid-January.

Without giving it much more thought, he replied, "Uh, sure guys. Let me grab my coat and shoes."

Hubert turned to find his things while Gabriel and Magdalena stood in the foyer. The Mueller's must not have been home as typically Betsy would have greeted them at the door in her pleasant demeanor.

Time seemed to stand still as Gabriel stood there with his hands in his pockets. As he gave a slight turn, he could see the door to Hubert's basement. It was located on the far side of the kitchen.

Gabriel felt a shiver run down his spine as he recalled the last time he was in that basement. They had just discovered the golden leaf book that had ultimately saved MALB from the demons of Lily Brooke's past.

"What are you thinking about, Gabriel?" inquired Magdalena.

She could tell that Gabriel's mood had changed. He didn't seem to be his relaxed self and was staring at Hubert's basement door.

As Gabriel turned to face Magdalena, she knew. He didn't even have to mutter a word.

A sense of guilt coursed through her veins as she too turned to eye the door. It was in that basement that Magdalena had learned she was a witch. Well, she had learned the possibility of being a witch.

MALB had sat around the round wooden table in Hubert's basement late last fall and had discovered that witches and wizards lived amongst the residents of Lily Brooke.

Before either one of them could utter a sound, Hubert re-appeared with his hair brushed, shoes on, and his coat buttoned up to face the wintry cold outside.

"Okay, let's go!" he curtly announced.

The friends headed out the front door and began the short walk to Hubert's barn.

Magdalena had always marveled at the fact the Mueller's home was so different than the barn. Of course, the barn was added years later after the house had been built, but the barn was your traditional bright red building as most were around the countryside. She just always thought it didn't seem to fit in with the castle-like ambiance of the house.

As they neared the barn entrance, the children knew Sugar Baby had sensed their arrival as the neighs and snorts were a welcoming sound.

Magdalena couldn't wait to throw her arms around the majestic animal. Sugar Baby had saved them more than once from the evil that lurked in the shadows of Lily Brooke. If it hadn't been for the athletic horse, MALB might have never survived the wrath of the demons.

As Magdalena jumped onto Sugar Baby's back, the horse seemed to purr like a cat.

Gabriel and Hubert laughed at Sugar Baby's enjoyment of seeing Magdalena. As the friends stood there for a few moments taking in the sight, Hubert realized there must be a reason for the little reunion on such a cold and wintery evening.

"So, I am going to assume you didn't miss Sugar Baby so bad that you walked to my house on such a cold wintery evening in January," stated Hubert.

The smiles quickly diminished as Magdalena sat upright on Sugar Baby's back.

"Are we alone, Hubert? Are your parents here tonight?" inquired Magdalena.

"Yes, we are alone. They went to the evening service at Saint Irmgardis. My mother had to work this morning, so my dad waited and attended the evening service with her," replied Hubert. "Why? What's going on?"

"I need to make some witchy soup," said Magdalena. "And, I need a few locks of hair from Sugar Baby in order to make that happen."

Hubert and Gabriel stood there like bumps on a log. Neither wanted to know the answer to what everyone in that barn knew would be the next question.

"Humor me, Mags, and explain why in the world you are making soup and why in the world you need horse hair? Better yet, I probably don't want to know," muttered Hubert.

Magdalena took a few moments to explain to Hubert about the book she had found in Leona's boutique. She talked about how she had been practicing some of the spells found inside of the book in case they ever came in handy. Living in Lily Brooke, you never knew when the next demon was hiding around the corner.

She further informed Hubert about the mason jar labeled 'twisted shrooms,' finding the little black book underneath the jar, and then discovering there was a spell titled 'twisted shrooms' inside the book.

Hubert was turning a little green, she noticed.

Of course, this was to be expected because out of all the MALB members, Hubert seemed to be the most uncomfortable with all the black magic around. This could have something to do with the fact he was almost a human sacrifice, she mused. It wasn't every day one was tied up by demons inside of a sacrificial cave and hung over a large bonfire. *He really did have reason to feel a little nauseous,* she thought.

"Magdalena, haven't we suffered enough adventures these past few months? I don't want to know why you want to make witchy soup, and I really don't care about a spell called twisted shrooms. I'm serious!" exclaimed Hubert.

Magdalena had been expecting this response and was well prepared for the rebuttal.

"Hubert, if the demons find a way to break out of the enchanted lanterns that we locked them inside of last fall, or there are more werewolves hiding in The Enchanted Forest, or if there is some evil force watching us, don't you want to be the most prepared we can be?" asked Magdalena.

She knew the way to Hubert's heart was through fear.

"Ugh, why do you do this to me? I thought you said we were safe from the demons and werewolves and everything else," cried Hubert. "Now, you are telling me they could come back?"

"Hubert, we have no idea what they can do. But the next time we encounter the dark forces hiding in the shadows, don't you want to be prepared?" suggested Magdalena.

Gabriel watched the ping pong conversation, and although he didn't want to be thrown into some other crazy adventure either, he knew that the one thing he could always guarantee was evil would find a way when there didn't seem to be a way. *Better to be prepared than desperate,* he thought. Besides, Gabriel had no black magic skills. He was a pure human.

Nothing special here, he surmised. *Better let Magdalena sharpen her spellcasting abilities.*

"So, not that I really want to know, but what is this soup you need to make?" gasped Hubert.

Gabriel tried hard to stifle the smile that spread across his lips. Boom! She had hooked Hubert, and before they knew it, Magdalena would have them in the next big adventure, whether they liked it or not. He had to admit; she was good at the art of persuasion.

Magdalena was so beautiful sitting on Sugar Baby's back. Her long brown hair glistened from the last sun rays peeping through the small barn window. The sun was almost completely gone for the day, but both Hubert and Gabriel couldn't miss her beauty as her face lit up in excitement as she began to disclose the secret found in chapter three of the little black book.

Grinning with excitement, Magdalena began to inform her two best friends of the secret recipe.

"Twisted shrooms is a potion that requires a mix of wild mushrooms, lily root, hair from a horse, garlic, and saliva of a witch or wizard. Once the ingredients are mixed, they must be cooked in a black cast iron cauldron," explained Magdalena.

"Gross," replied Hubert. "You mean to tell me you have to spit in the soup? Yuck! You won't catch me drinking that stuff."

"Hubert, you will be surprised what you may drink if the demons show back up," laughed Gabriel.

On the inside, it didn't seem to be very funny to him. But at the moment, it was quite comical watching Hubert process Magdalena's words.

Hubert just glared at Gabriel as he knew he did have a valid point.

Magdalena was petting Sugar Baby on the back of the neck while giving the boys time to let it all sink in.

"Hubert, do you have any scissors? I want to cut some of Sugar Baby's mane to keep with me," said Magdalena.

Hubert walked over to the storage box, where they kept flashlights, rope, and other miscellaneous items in the barn. He dug through and found a pair of old shears.

"Here you go, Mags."

Magdalena took the shears from Hubert's outstretched hand and whispered into Sugar Baby's ear.

"I'm going to cut a small piece of your hair, Sugar Baby, for a spell that will protect us all against the evil hiding in Lily Brooke. It won't hurt, I promise."

The horse seemed to sense and understand Magdalena's words. She had been trained as Lily Brooke's first line of defense against the dark side. Sugar Baby stood at attention while Magdalena cut a few lockets of hair and gently placed it in her jeans' pocket.

Hubert replaced the shears in the storage box, and Magdalena slid down off the horse to stand eye level with Gabriel and Hubert.

Knowing he didn't want to hear her response, but also realizing it was a must, Gabriel inquired, "So Mags, what does this twisted shrooms spell do, and why do we need it?"

She had been waiting for the ultimate question, wondering how long it would take the boys to realize there was a significant reason this specific spell was of so much importance. But she also knew she had to feed them little snippets of information at a time so as to not overwhelm them all at once.

Guarding her response, she replied, "You bring the soup to a boil and let it simmer for exactly one hour. The potion will turn bright purple, begin to foam, and talks to you. This is when you know the potion is ready."

Hubert and Gabriel gave each other the look of painful recognition. They both knew this wasn't going to end well for either one of them.

"What do you mean when you say the potion 'talks to you'?" whispered Gabriel. He could feel his stomach twist into a knot.

"Yeah, Mags, you know I don't do spooky, so whatever you mean by the soup talking to us, well, you can just tell that soup to shut up!" exclaimed Hubert.

For a second, Magdalena thought Hubert was going to turn and run from the barn, leaving her and Gabriel on their own. She could sense he was one foot already out of the barn. But she also knew Hubert was prideful. As much as he was easily spooked and didn't handle scary situations very well, he was also equally prideful and would never abandon his friends in a time of need.

"Hubert, I wasn't a hundred percent correct when I said the potion would talk to us when it was ready," replied Magdalena.

"Oh, thank goodness," responded Hubert. "I mean, I just can't do some spooky talking soup spell."

Thinking he had successfully diverted a very difficult and ridiculously freaky situation, he let out a big sigh.

Gabriel knew better. He knew Mags was about to pounce.

"Uh Hubert, I meant when the soup potion was ready, we would be able to hear the witches' screams."

And with that last statement, she brought down the barn.

As Hubert was frantically pacing the barn and speaking in what sounded like some foreign language, Magdalena and Gabriel watched in a stupor. They all knew Hubert didn't handle fear very well, but this was a whole new level of panic.

When Hubert seemed to be winding down from exhaustion, Magdalena approached him and got his attention by standing about a foot in front of him.

"Hubert, it's all going to be okay. We couldn't have made it this far without you. You are my rock. None of us asked for the events that have transacted these last few months. But, we have no choice other than to arm ourselves with every resource available. We never know what we could encounter in the future," explained Magdalena.

Hubert knew she was right, but that didn't make the news any easier.

"I know, Mags. I'm just tired of being spooked and haunted," whispered Hubert. "I miss the days of feeling normal and doing normal kid things. I mean seriously, I just want to lay around the house in my pajamas all day and not worry about a demon jumping through my bedroom window!"

"Hubert, I'm with you, man. But I would rather be in the room with Magdalena and her black magic skills, than alone without her when the demons call," negotiated Gabriel.

"Yes, me, too!" exclaimed Hubert.

"I have a suggestion," offered Magdalena. "Let's round up the rest of MALB and meet at the old tire swing in a few hours to discuss this book and what it means to our future and defending Lily Brooke."

"Sounds good to me," said Gabriel. "But Mags, you never said what the twisted shrooms spell is used for or what it actually does."

Magdalena stood there quietly as she tried to find the right words. She knew the boys were completely spooked, and she didn't want to divulge too much information before she had a chance to meet with the gang.

"Let's just say this would have been a great spell to know when we took a ride over the slippery slope a few weeks ago," grinned Magdalena.

Gabriel and Hubert exchanged glances, not knowing anything more than they did a few seconds ago.

With that, Magdalena turned and walked out of the barn. She was on a mission to find Greta, Piper, and Cody before the sun completely set on what was turning out to be yet another mysterious day in Lily Brooke.

MALB REUNITES
~ Four ~

After leaving the barn, the friends decided to divide and conquer. Magdalena would find Greta while Gabriel would locate Cody, and Hubert would find Piper. All agreed to meet at the old tire swing by the oak tree within the hour.

Only Magdalena knew what lay ahead of the friend group, but she was keeping it tight-lipped until everyone was back together.

Gabriel wasn't sure if Magdalena being so secretive, had him more or less confident at what may be actually cooking up in this witchy soup. Nonetheless, he knew the first order of business was to find his friends. So, off to Cody's house, he went.

Gabriel stood at Cody's front door, ringing the doorbell. He was beginning to think the Malik family must not be home when suddenly the door flung open with Cody standing there out of breath, holding the most adorable two-toned beagle pup.

"Hey man, sorry it took me so long to get to the door. Mac just decided it would be the perfect time to bolt down the basement steps when the doorbell rang," panted Cody, obviously a little more out of breath than he would have liked to admit.

Gabriel chuckled while giving Mac a pet on top of the head.

"That's okay, Cody, no problem. I almost thought no one was home," replied Gabriel.

"Just Mac and I right now. Want to come inside out of the cold?"

"Well, actually, I just wanted to see if you were available for a MALB meeting this evening. Magdalena is up to her old tricks and a few new ones and has requested for everyone to meet at the oak tree," informed Gabriel.

"Oh, boy, not again. Dude, not again!" exclaimed Cody.

Gabriel knew Cody wasn't really looking for a response and that he was just processing the same panic that he and Hubert had felt moments ago inside of Hubert's barn.

"The only thing I can tell you is she is carrying lockets of horsehair, Sugar Baby's to be exact, in her pocket and hiding a little black spellbook inside of her coat," said Gabriel.

Cody turned ash white, and Gabriel couldn't stifle his laughter. He knew those words would get Cody moving a little quicker.

"Let me grab my coat and Mac's leash, and I will be ready to go," whispered Cody in such a faint tone that Gabriel had to strain to hear his words.

Not realizing what he had done, Cody ran to grab his things as the front door quickly slammed shut in Gabriel's face.

He stood there thinking nothing of it, as he knew his friend was feeling the same emotions that they were all feeling.

Within a few minutes, Cody was locking the front door behind them with Mac attached to his leash. Without another word, the two boys and adorable pup headed towards the old oak tree.

Magdalena was passing by Adolphe's bakery on the way to Greta's house and happened to notice she was inside chatting with Adolphe.

As the door to Adolphe's shop opened, the little bell rang, announcing a new visitor. Greta and Adolphe both looked up and greeted their friend as they saw her familiar face.

"Magdalena, it is so good to see you. I have something new for you to try. Hang on, don't move, I will be right back," ushered Adolphe.

Knowing she would never get out of the little bakery without tasting one of Adolphe's new food creations, Magdalena just smiled as she saw the little chef disappear behind the swinging doors.

"Hello, Greta. I was just on my way to your house and saw you inside. It's so good to see you," smiled Magdalena, and she gave her friend a warm embrace.

"Oh, really, what's up, Mags?" inquired Greta.

As excited as she was to see her childhood friend, she knew something must be up for Magdalena to be seeking her out on this cold January evening.

Looking around to be sure no one could hear their conversation, Magdalena replied, "We are going to have a MALB meeting at the old oak tree this evening, and I am hoping you can join."

Greta could feel the hair on her arms stand up. She knew something was up now. The gang wouldn't be getting together on such a cold and wintery day, in the evening nonetheless. Her stomach began to flip, and now she didn't feel hungry at all, even for Adolphe's amazing pastries.

"If you wait for just a second, I can walk with you to the oak tree. I just need to pay Adolphe for the cinnamon pastry," said Greta.

Whatever Magdalena had up her sleeve, Greta would be there to support her friend. Not wanting another adventure but also not wanting to be constantly looking over her shoulder, Greta knew she had no choice but to join the gang.

Before another word could be spoken, Adolphe flew through the bakery doors waving a light blue iced donut. As he placed the donut in Magdalena's hands, she noticed the detail work.

Adolphe had managed to bake a light blue donut that featured intricate thin white icing in the shape of a hand-drawn snowflake.

"Goodness, Adolphe, this is too beautiful to eat!" exclaimed Magdalena.

"Yes, yes, yes, please eat! I want to know what you think of the taste. Share some with Greta, and let's see what both of you think."

Adolphe looked like a child on Christmas morning. He was always so anxious, yet overwhelmingly excited to launch a new food item. And he knew the children would be honest with him and let him know if he needed to keep perfecting the recipe, or if it was ready for the bakery showcase.

Magdalena took a bite, and it seemed as though a burst of wintery goodness exploded in her mouth. She felt herself begin to melt.

Adolphe, obviously very thrilled with the results even though she had yet to speak, began rushing Greta to go ahead and have a taste.

Greta took a piece of the donut from Magdalena and, too, began to eat. She smiled with big bright eyes, and Adolphe knew he had hit a home run.

Both girls seemed to find their voice at the same time, and both exclaimed, "It's amazing!"

Giggling at the same choice of words, the two couldn't get another word in as Adolphe ran into the back of the store with his arms flailing and shouting words of thanks as he went to get the rest of the snowflake donuts to add to the showcase.

Greta laid the dollar for the cinnamon pastry she had purchased on the counter by the register as in Adolphe's excitement, he had forgotten to take her payment.

The girls turned and left the bakery feeling warm and fuzzy on the inside because no matter what was going on in life, seeing Adolphe excited and proud was something that warmed one's heart. Adolphe had been supplying Lily Brooke with his handmade food creations for years, and well, he always had a way of reminding one that sometimes it is the simple things in life that mean the most.

Magdalena and Greta walked in tandem headed towards the old oak tree.

Hubert was grumbling all the way to Piper's house. He absolutely couldn't believe that Magdalena was about to launch them into another ridiculous, scary situation right after Christmas. For goodness sake, it had only been a few weeks since the last living nightmare he had survived.

But there was something about Magdalena that just wouldn't allow him to say no. And, he knew that. This seemed to irritate him more than the fact he was about to learn about something like witchy soup.

Hubert arrived at Piper Baer's house and rang the doorbell. He waited a few moments and then tried again. Still no answer. Not wanting to disappoint Magdalena, Hubert walked around to the back of the house just in case Piper was outside and didn't hear the doorbell.

Sure enough, Piper was outside making a snowman with his little neighbor. Hubert felt his stance soften as they watched the little boy from next door giggle and laugh while Piper helped him add the carrot nose to the lopsided snowman.

Piper noticed Hubert and waved him over.

"Hey, Hubert! Good to see you! Want to join in the snowman fun?" asked Piper.

"I would love to but looks like you are all done," responded Hubert.

"Well, I guess that is a good point," said Piper. He could sense that Hubert must have had something serious on his mind.

Turning to his neighbor, Piper said, "Thank you for helping me build the snowman today, Johnny. You better get inside now before you turn into a snowman, too."

At that, little Johnny laughed and gave Piper a nice big hug.

"Come over if you want my mom to make you some warm hot chocolate," yelled Johnny as he ran to his back door, not waiting to hear a response.

Once Johnny was back inside, Piper turned to Hubert and said, "Did you just come to visit, or has something happened?"

Piper could feel his insides start to turn to mush and was hoping Hubert had just stopped by for a friendly visit. Somehow, he knew better.

"Mags and Gabriel wanted me to find you and meet at the old oak tree," replied Hubert. "You don't want to know, man. You don't want to know."

With Hubert's words hanging over like dark snow clouds, Piper knew he had no option but to head towards the club's hiding spot.

"Then let's go!" replied Piper. "I just hope it is only MALB meeting at the old oak tree and not the demons of Lily Brooke's past."

All of the MALB members arrived at the old oak tree at about the same time. Magdalena and Greta, Cody and Gabriel, Hubert, and Piper.

As they all saw each other, a round of hugs and salutations began as they all hadn't been together since the week before Christmas when they had journeyed home from Lindtzl Kingdom.

As the excitement began to wear off, daylight was almost completely gone, and the air was shivering cold, so Hubert suggested they gather firewood and get a fire going as it could be a long evening.

The friends worked together and got a nice campfire roaring with heat as they sat around the circle together, warming their bodies.

The nostalgia wasn't lost on any of them, as this was precisely how the last adventure had begun.

Hubert cleared his throat and brought the official meeting to order.

"Everyone around the circle officially state your name in attendance for the record," he ordered.

"Magdalena Gottschalk."

"Gabriel Bach."

"Cody Malik and Mac."

"Piper Baer."

"Greta Ishmehl."

"Hubert Mueller."

"All names have been accepted and welcome to the club, Mac," snickered Hubert. "Hey, you never know when a cute beagle pup will be needed."

The gang had a good laugh while everyone came over to pet Mac's head. The little beagle seemed to love the attention.

"At least he now listens to small commands," said Cody.

"Ah, he will be a great addition," piped Gabriel. And on a serious note, you didn't know when extra reinforcement would be needed around Lily Brooke. Sugar Baby had been a savior to the gang, and who knew, maybe little Mac would have his day, too.

Everyone settled back down and took their place by the campfire. It was now dark, eerie, and very cold. The friends sat close to the fire, trying to keep warm.

Knowing everyone had the burning question on their mind, Greta addressed the group.

"Magdalena, what brings us here today? I missed everyone over the holidays, but I'm sure this isn't a celebratory meeting."

Magdalena had been contemplating how to inform her friends about everything without completely spooking them first. Somehow, she just didn't think that was possible.

Clearing her throat, Magdalena dove in and began the story.

"I began working for my mother's boutique over the holiday break and came across a little black book hidden on a shelf in her storeroom. This book is special as it is full of secret spells."

"Stop there, Mags!" shouted Piper. "We don't need to know about any spells. The demons are locked up, and their gatekeeper werewolf spell was broken."

She was hoping to get further along in the story before the panic hit but realized tiptoeing wasn't going to work this time.

"I wasn't going to tell everyone I have been working on learning some of the ancient secret spells using my black magic skills. It was something I was just going to do on my own in case a time ever arose that I needed the knowledge. But Gabriel happened to catch me working on a levitation spell," replied Magdalena.

No one spoke a word, not even Gabriel, so she continued.

"Anyway, I'll explain more about that spell later. Gabriel convinced me I should return the book to my mother's store before she noticed it missing, so we went to her boutique to return the book. As I went to replace it under the jar labeled 'twisted shrooms' on the shelf where I had found it, with Gabriel's help, it occurred to me that twisted shrooms sounded like something maybe I should investigate."

"Gee, thanks, man! Couldn't you just let it go?" barked Hubert as he looked straight at Gabriel.

"Sorry guys, I regretted it as soon as it left my lips," smiled Gabriel.

Magdalena ignored the rebuttal and continued.

"I opened the little black book again and noticed there was a spell titled 'twisted shrooms.' This is why you are here."

"Well, Mags, I hate to bring up the obvious, but you are the only one of us that can do anything with a spell. Why do you need us, and what makes this spell so special?" inquired Cody.

Magdalena could hear several of her friends mutter similar thoughts, so she pushed on.

"I know guys; this seems terrifying after our last two ordeals. But we don't get to pick and choose when evil seeks us out. We are the protectors of Lily Brooke, and although we never wanted any of this bestowed upon us, we are responsible for making sure the evil forces in Lily Brooke's past don't come back," pleaded Magdalena.

Although no one wanted to hear it, they all agreed. No one had a choice.

"Okay, Mags, tell us more," grumbled Hubert.

"Twisted Shrooms is a spell that combines wild mushrooms, lily root, hair from a horse, garlic, and saliva from a witch or wizard. The concoction is then cooked for one hour exactly in a cast-iron cauldron. When this witchy soup is ready, it will turn a bright purple foam, and you will hear witch screams in the mix."

Magdalena stopped speaking and let the words hang over her friends for a few moments. She knew this would be the first big hurdle in today's debriefing.

"Oh my God, I can't," replied Cody. "There is no way I want to see some witch soup that screams. Seriously, Mags!"

"Calm down, everyone, calm down," said Gabriel. "Let's see where Magdalena is going with this."

Magdalena continued. "This potion is very important and would have come in very handy in our last adventure down the slippery slope. When drank, the potion allows hidden vortexes to be seen. Remember, we knew we had flown through a hidden vortex but couldn't escape The Enchanted Forest because we couldn't see the vortex. Well, this spell will allow me to see where they exist. Not only can we identify them, but it gives us the ability to travel between human populations and enchanted areas."

"I definitely see how this would be a very important skill to have," said Greta. "But we are done with the scary demonic just plain weird adventures, Magdalena. This would have been helpful in the past, but we are all clear now."

"We hope we are all clear now," retorted Hubert. "But did anyone plan on flying over the slippery slope last month to be chased by a three-headed werewolf? I didn't think so. I don't like this AT ALL either! But if I have no choice and evil is going to pop up out of the blue all the time, I would rather Magdalena be prepared."

"Ugh, I hate when you make sense, Hubert, but I hate anything regarding black magic worse," whispered Piper. He had already lost his voice from fear.

Magdalena watched her friends debate the importance of her practicing and learning this spell. She knew the internal conflict they all shared, as she also felt the same way. However, she knew she had a duty to the town of Lily Brooke, and no matter how scared she felt, she had to embrace her life's calling and understood well her place in the community was as a protector. She must arm herself with every trick, spell, and potion available to protect her community, friends, and family.

After a few more moments of the debate, Hubert cleared his throat and addressed the group.

"We now need to take a group vote. All in favor of supporting Magdalena and this witchy soup stuff, state your name."

"Hubert Mueller."

"Gabriel Bach."

It sat quietly for a few moments, and Hubert thought this might be the first time that MALB didn't get a unanimous vote.

"Greta Ishmehl."

"Piper Baer."

"Cody Malik and Mac."

The air hung heavy over the heads of MALB, but it was settled.

"Anyone up for a game of Royals and Robbers?" giggled Magdalena.

What better way to soften the news and enjoy her friends for a little while, she thought.

"Yeah!" shouted Hubert. He was definitely ready for some light-hearted fun.

"Count me in!" responded Piper. *This was more like it,* he thought.

Not another thought about demons, witches, or wizards occurred, and the MALB members spent the next hour having a blast living in the moment. They all knew they were way too old to be playing a mock game of hide-and-go-seek, but they didn't care. It was like old times.

The fire began to dwindle, and the friends were getting cold.

"Mags, I can walk you home on my way if you like," said Gabriel.

"Sure, I would love that," said Magdalena whole-heartedly. She honestly hoped the fun they had this evening would help Gabriel return to his normal self. She didn't like the distance she was feeling from him, which was something she hadn't experienced before.

After making sure the fire was extinguished, the gang headed their separate ways as Monday morning would be here before they knew it.

Gabriel walked Magdalena home and watched her walk through the little white picket fence gate to her front door. Once she had gone inside and closed the door, he headed home.

SKULLY RETURNS
~ Five ~

Magdalena was grateful for the hot shower and felt relaxed and thankful while she slipped into her pink silk pajamas. They were her absolute favorite, and after the day she had, she wanted a comfortable night of sleep.

She jumped beneath the covers and felt the softness of her pillow as she geared up for some good sleep.

She laid there listening to how quiet the house was, not even a tick of the clock or creak in the night.

Allison, her little sister, had gone to bed earlier that night, and Magdalena figured her parents must now be in bed, too.

She closed her eyes and willed herself to sleep, but thirty minutes later, she was still lying there wide awake.

Irritated with herself, she began to toss and turn, not understanding why she couldn't fall asleep.

After another fifteen minutes or so, Magdalena realized the reason she couldn't fall asleep. Her sixth sense had been heightened. She couldn't shake the feeling that danger was near.

Not knowing why she jumped out of bed to view out her bedroom window. She stood there in the darkness, trying to figure out why the strong sense of evil felt so near.

After a few moments, she shrugged it off and decided it must be her mind playing tricks on her. It had been quite spooky at the old oak tree tonight with all the talk of demons and spells.

Feeling a little silly, Magdalena climbed back into bed, and this time fell asleep within minutes.

She couldn't have been asleep long when she sat straight up in the bed. Asleep or not, she knew the unmistakable sound outside of her bedroom window. The panic and fear that shot through her had her on her feet and dressed within seconds.

Standing at her bedroom window clothed in jeans, her favorite hooded sweatshirt, and boots, Magdalena gently pulled the curtain back from the side to peek outside.

She didn't see anything and wondered if it had all been a dream.

Then, the unmistakable howl cut through the night like hot magma exploding from a volcano.

Her mind went straight to the moment in time when she heard this sound before. Evil had been lurking in the shadows waiting on her to follow the noise. The three-headed werewolf had been waiting behind the tree at the edge of the slippery slope. It had been waiting to push her off the edge and send her down the treacherous terrain to her death.

But she had survived, and the events that unfolded from that moment forward had her hiding behind her bedroom curtain shivering in fear.

As her mind began to clear, she realized the sound was the same, but the curse had been beaten. The werewolf was no longer a werewolf; it was now a dog. And not only was it a pet dog, but it was also by Queen Lindtzl's side in Lindtzl Kingdom.

Something had to be wrong. It absolutely had to be Skully that Magdalena was hearing howl in the night. But there was no way that Skully could have found where she lived in Lily Brooke. It was so far away from Lindtzl Kingdom.

Realizing she had to investigate and hoping this wasn't some evil trick from another demon on the loose, Magdalena carefully and quietly raised her bedroom window. She grabbed the wrought iron ladder that was attached to the backside of the house.

A smile slid across her face as she remembered the ladder had been a gift from Gabriel. He had made it with his bare hands in his dad's blacksmith shop. That ladder meant more to her than any earthly possession.

Magdalena was careful to hold on tight to the sides of the ladder as she slowly descended and landed on the ground.

She took a look around and didn't see anything amiss. It was a crystal-clear night, cold and brisk, with a full moon in the sky.

Wondering what to do now, Magdalena turned to head around the side of the house and saw Skully standing there in front of her, tail wagging and eyes as big as saucers.

Skully was quite a sight for sore eyes. Magdalena wrapped her arms around the three-headed dog's neck, well formerly werewolf's neck. Skully gave Magdalena's cheek a few good licks, and the tail was rapidly wagging back and forth.

"It is soooo good to see you, Skully!" Magdalena whispered in the animal's ear.

As she leaned back to stand up, she noticed a plastic tube hanging around the dog's neck with a hand-written note inside.

Magdalena removed the note carefully and was able to read clearly by the light of the full moon.

The letter was from the queen herself, and she begged MALB to pay her a visit. She mentioned she didn't want to disclose the reasons why in case the letter fell into the wrong hands but said it was of the most urgent matter. Queen Lindtzl told Magdalena to come fully armed, ready for battle, with any resources she could muster.

Panicked and worried for the queen, Magdalena felt there was very little time. She told Skully to stay while she climbed back up the ladder to her bedroom.

She slid her hand beneath her mattress and pulled out the little black book. She now desperately wished she had gotten further along in the book of spells, but at least she could take it with her as a reference in case black magic was needed.

Almost forgetting the most important of all, she walked back inside of her closet, grabbed the snow globe that had been a gift from the queen, and opened her jewelry chest. She had managed to create a hidden compartment inside. She opened the bottom drawer and removed the black felt lining the drawer. Underneath where the felt had laid, was a wooden insert.

Magdalena carefully removed the insert and opened the small box adorned in jewels. She quickly peeked inside to find the one thing the demons had hoped to take from her. She found the golden leaf.

Even standing there in the dim closet room, she could see the etched beauty in the figurine. Knowing this leaf held the key of all power in Lily Brooke, Magdalena felt it might help save Lindtzl Kingdom. She replaced the golden leaf inside of the gemmed box and hid it inside of her sweatshirt front pocket.

Magdalena grabbed her most prized locket from the inside of the jewelry chest as well, opened it quickly to make sure there was still dried lily root inside, and put it around her neck, hiding it underneath the sweatshirt.

Her most important possessions, the locket, the golden leaf, and the little black book was all she had to offer the queen. But she was going to give it everything she had, as the queen had saved their lives, and they would be eternally grateful.

Quickly finding a pen, Magdalena wrote a note to Gabriel instructing him to wake up Cody, Greta, and Piper and to meet her at Hubert's barn. She let Gabriel know it was an emergency and to please hurry.

Once satisfied with the note, she climbed back down the ladder and placed the note to Gabriel in the plastic tube around Skully's neck.

"Skully, I need you to find Gabriel and make sure he sees this note. He is to meet me at Hubert's barn with the others," she whispered into the dog's ear.

With no time to worry about whether the plan would work, Magdalena ran off in the other direction to get to Hubert's. She was having a hard time figuring out how she would wake him up without alerting the Mueller's. Hubert wasn't exactly a light sleeper. It was a task she would just have to figure out when she got there.

Skully knew Queen Lindtzl depended on him, so the three-headed dog ran as fast as it could to Gabriel's. Once there, it only took one howl outside of Gabriel's window to alert him.

As Gabriel peered out his window and saw Skully, he knew Magdalena must be in trouble as it wasn't difficult to figure out that Skully would have gone to Magdalena and not him if it were just a visit.

Gabriel dressed as quickly as he could and was outside his bedroom window, leaning down in front of Skully within what seemed like seconds.

He pulled Magdalena's note from the tube around the dog's neck and felt the jolt of fear course through his veins. Without another thought, Gabriel and Skully headed off into the night to round up the Mystical Alliance of Lily Brooke.

Magdalena arrived at the corner of Wildwood Lane and got that old familiar twinge in her stomach as she saw the façade of the Mueller home in the light of the full moon. She would never visit that house without her sixth sense kicking into overdrive.

Well, no time for that, she thought.

Magdalena sprinted down Wildwood Lane and made a sharp turn to go around the back of Hubert's house. His bedroom was on the second story of the massive home. With no way to climb up to his window, she stood there, pondering how to wake him up.

Before Magdalena had another thought, Hubert raised his window and shouted out below, "What are you doing here, Magdalena? It's late!"

Magdalena must have jumped a foot in the air as she could hear Hubert laugh for a brief moment.

"I need to talk to you, Hubert. It's an emergency!" she replied.

"Okay! Come on up," he replied.

"I can't. There isn't a ladder or any way up there," she responded.

"Um, Mags, aren't you a witch? You have flown before," smirked Hubert.

Magdalena felt like a black cloud had moved and almost felt a little dumb. Here stood Hubert at the top of the second-story window, reminding her she was a witch and could fly if needed. She had been so preoccupied trying to figure out how to climb; she forgot to use her black magic skills.

Magdalena pulled the locket from underneath her sweatshirt, held it in her hand, and spoke.

"Lily root, lily root, agent of the night, help me fly away, fly away, like a bird in the night."

Magdalena opened her eyes as she began to float through the air up to Hubert's bedroom window. Once inside, she tucked the locket back underneath her shirt.

"Hubert, how did you know I was standing outside of your room?" she panted. For the life of her, she couldn't figure out how Hubert knew she had been standing there.

"It's weird actually," he whispered. "I haven't been able to sleep much tonight. I think you must have scared the bejeezus out of me tonight talking about demons and twisted shrooms or whatever you were talking about. I have tossed and turned all night. I just can't seem to get rid of the feeling that something evil is lurking around here," he replied.

Magdalena wondered if Hubert's intuition was the beginning of his spiritual coming of age season. She had wondered if he was truly a pure human, or if he would turn out to be a wizard. Having both a witch and wizard for parents would seem to present the condition that Hubert was most definitely a wizard.

But Magdalena knew spiritual hearing, as the enchanted world called it, was something that didn't typically manifest in a child until late teen to young adulthood years. Hubert was just thirteen, and Magdalena was the second child in all of Lily Brooke's history to experience it at such a young age.

"I had the same night as you, Hubert. I couldn't sleep either. I'm here because Queen Lindtzl needs our help!" exclaimed Magdalena.

Hubert looked at Magdalena and had a million questions for her. But it only took one look to realize she was very serious.

"What do we need to do, Mags?"

"We need to get to your barn. Skully is on his way to round up Gabriel and the others. We can talk there and put forth a plan to help save the queen," she said.

Without arguing, Hubert ran to his bedroom closet, shut the door, and quickly changed out of his pajamas into something warmer.

Within seconds, Magdalena found herself and Hubert quietly tiptoeing through the house to get to the front door. Magdalena couldn't help but shoot a quick glance at the Mueller's basement door as she went right past it. *Not so great memories there,* she thought.

Hubert grabbed Magdalena by the hand, and they were off running to the barn before she could blink.

As they entered the barn, Magdalena heard Sugar Baby before she rounded the corner.

Sugar Baby must have sensed the panic in Magdalena, and she came over to nestle her nose on the side of Magdalena's face.

With love, Magdalena buried her face against the horse's long snout. She knew if anyone understood how she felt at that moment, it would be the stallion.

The barn door slowly opened, and in came Skully, Gabriel, Cody and Mac, Piper, and Greta.

Magdalena threw her arms around Skully's neck and thanked the dog over and over for completing its mission.

"Magdalena, what has happened?" whispered Greta so out of breath, she almost couldn't mumble.

"Everyone, please, come in closer," responded Magdalena. "I have a message from Queen Lindtzl that Skully delivered to me tonight."

Taking a deep breath, she continued to read the queen's letter.

As Magdalena finished the letter, she folded it back up and slipped into her jeans' pocket for safekeeping.

"This doesn't sound good," replied Cody. "There is no way I want to go back to that crazy forest with the haunted castle and eerie rules."

"Ditto," replied Piper. "But, I don't think we have the option considering that the queen sounds so desperate."

"Agreed," said Gabriel. "It sounds as if maybe the demons have been freed from captivity. She was afraid her letter might fall into the hands of the wrong person or thing, which has me a little worried."

"I'm not going back. I'm serious. There is no way you will get me to go back to that enchanted place. Nope. Not doing it," replied Hubert.

"Yes, the queen sounds very desperate to me, and I am going to help her. I was hoping all of you would come with me. I can't do this without all of you. But I completely understand, Hubert, if you don't want to go," voiced Magdalena.

Hubert didn't want to have anything to do with the slippery slope or the hidden vortex or anything else that revolved around Lindtzl Kingdom. He was done with this spooky stuff. But he also cared very deeply for Magdalena, and the thought of not being by her side in a moment of danger was worse to him than the fear bubbled up inside of his soul.

"Do you think the queen will have that table of food spread out again?" asked Hubert.

Well, that was all it took to break the silence in the barn. No matter how scared they were, Hubert and his hunger pains were something they all could laugh about.

"Hubert, I'm sure the queen will make sure you are well fed. And, I wouldn't want to do this without you," replied Magdalena.

Feeling like the jerk of the group, Hubert said, "And, you won't have to. But Mags, better keep those black screaming witchy soup skills or spells handy this time as I'm not chasing or running from no demons or werewolves again! I mean it!"

Magdalena was overjoyed that once again, the gang would be back together in yet another adventure. She just secretly hoped they wouldn't be up against something they couldn't handle.

"You guys know what to do," sang Magdalena as she removed the beautiful snow globe from the front pocket of her hoodie sweatshirt.

Each of the friends took in the beautiful scene of them having dinner in the winter wonderland right outside of the queen's castle. Hubert was salivating at the display of food found from one end of the table to the other. The Christmas lights adorned the snow-covered trees, and it reminded each of them of the spirit of Christmas and how amazing their parting of ways with the queen had been. She had gifted them this snow globe, so they would remember their time there together and could visit any time they wished.

Well, this wouldn't be a pleasure trip, but the gang was ready to see the queen and determine what was happening yet again in Lindtzl Kingdom.

After gently shaking it, Magdalena held the globe out in front of her while the rest of the friends made a circle around the globe, laying their hands atop the globe. Magdalena took Skully's paw and laid it to rest on top of her own hand.

"Everyone close your eyes," whispered Magdalena, "and be sure to leave your hand on the globe. If you break contact with the globe, you won't make the journey," she warned.

"Snow globe, snow globe, take us through the night to visit Queen Lindtzl in her kingdom," chanted Magdalena.

Within a few seconds, Sugar Baby and the other Mueller horses remained standing in the barn, all alone.

The gang landed softly on the newly fallen snow. As they opened their eyes, they couldn't believe the sight that unfolded before them. What had been the most beautiful winter wonderland they had ever seen or imagined, was now a rotting wasteland.

The friends were all at a loss for words and just stood there, staring at the grim view in front of them.

The table that had proudly hosted the feast last December was now rotting and covered with rats, mice, and other undistinguishable rodents. Flies and maggots were oozing from the left-over food lying on the serving plates from one end of the table to the other.

Hubert especially couldn't believe what he was witnessing. It truly broke his heart to see the devastation. The queen had prepared such a glorious event for the children right before they returned home. To see the waste, to see the fungus and mold growing all over the table, was heartbreaking.

As the children moved their gaze from the table to the surrounding area, it didn't take long to see that the beautiful winter kissed wonderland they had left was now a disaster.

The Christmas lights that had hung so brightly from the large evergreen snow-covered trees were all busted and left to dangle in disarray from the broken branches.

It looked as though some type of evil storm had spun without control throughout the land all around them.

Magdalena felt the tears well up beneath her green eyes. *How could this be?* She thought. And more importantly, *what has happened to the queen?*

Gabriel took one look at Magdalena's face and knew he would have to be the one to stand tall for his best friend. He saw the hurt, he saw the guilt, and he knew she would blame herself for leaving the queen alone to do battle with the unknown.

"Mags, this isn't your fault. This isn't our fault. We happened upon this land after the feud in these lands had transpired. When we left here, the queen was getting to go back home and live in her castle. I don't know what has happened here, but we didn't cause this," said Gabriel in the most soft-spoken voice Greta thought she had ever witnessed.

"What is that smell?" screeched Hubert. "I can't stand it. What is it?"

Everyone had been overwhelmed by the smell of pure evil.

"I think that is the smell of rotting food and rotting kingdom," said Piper with a jaw so locked you almost couldn't decipher his words.

"This is so awful. How will we find the queen? I'm afraid something terrible has happened to her," teared Greta.

Cody was holding Mac as tight as he could. He was scared to put the pup down for fear he might ingest some type of poison, or worse.

"Wait, I have an idea where we can find the queen!" exclaimed Cody.

All eyes turned to see what Cody had in mind. At this point, any idea was welcome as the sight before them was one they were ready to leave.

"Door number two, remember? If we follow this path, it leads to one of the exit doors from Lindtzl Castle," suggested Cody.

"He's right!" shouted Magdalena. How could she forget?

"Tunnel number two in the dungeon led to the frozen steel door. Remember, guys? We shined the flashlight on the frozen door, and it opened, leading us to what was a beautiful winter wonderland. Let's go!"

Before everyone could process Magdalena's words, she was off running as fast as she could. She wanted to get away from the stench and decay and find the queen.

Everyone caught up with Magdalena, and they reached the steel door. Magdalena tried to turn the handle, and the door didn't budge.

Each MALB member took their turn, trying to pry open the steel door.

"The queen must have locked the door from the inside of the castle to make sure no one could sneak in from this secret entrance," stated Piper. "Now, what?"

"Why don't we try to shine a light on the outside of the door and see if we can activate the handle the same way as we did on the inside?" inquired Cody.

"Great idea! Does anyone have a flashlight?" asked Gabriel.

"I do," responded Hubert. "I brought rope, three flashlights, and a pair of shears."

In Magdalena's haste to get out of Hubert's barn, she hadn't thought to bring additional resources with them. It sure was a good thing Hubert had thought about it, or they would be standing in this evil forsaken forest with nothing but a locket, jeweled box, snow globe, and little black book.

"Thank goodness for you, Hubert. I was so focused on convincing everyone to come along for the adventure to help the queen that I forgot to get any supplies," murmured Magdalena.

"Oh, it's okay, Mags, I got your back," smiled Hubert. *Score one for Hubert,* he thought. Maybe one day, Magdalena would notice that he was more useful than just as a friend.

Hubert pulled out the three flashlights and gave one to himself, Gabriel, and Cody. The three of them began concentrating the light energy onto the handle of door number two.

After a few moments of directing all the light they had onto the door, and each saying a little individual prayer, Hubert tried to open the door.

It didn't budge — not even an inch.

"How can we find the queen? It didn't work? Mags, what do we do? Find some black magic or come up with some witchy soup, or something!" cried Hubert in one of the most frantic voices Magdalena thought she had ever heard.

Magdalena stood there, staring at Hubert's distraught expression, not knowing what to say.

All she could muster was, "Maybe everything we need is in this Christmas gift of love."

"Do what?" asked Greta. "I'm not seeing much love here, Mags."

"Oh, but there is beauty inside of everything. You just have to know where to look," smiled Magdalena.

THE SNOW GLOBE
~ Six ~

Magdalena instructed everyone to softly lay one hand on the snow globe while concentrating their gaze to the scene in front of them.

Hubert thought Magdalena must have lost her mind because staring at the beautiful winter wonderland setting inside of the snow globe didn't do anything but remind him of what it looked like right now. He couldn't imagine how this did anything for the predicament in which they now found themselves.

"Mags, you know I trust you. But reminding us that we are now stuck in an evil enchanted forest with rotting food and who knows what lurks around the corner isn't going to help anything. I don't need to sit and stare at what this placed used to look like. I just want to find the queen and get out of here," demanded Hubert.

Magdalena realized she must be the only one to have taken the queen's words seriously. But then again, Magdalena was known as being the brightest and most intelligent of the group. She was just wired that way. She drove her teachers nuts at school because she was always the one to question the inner-workings of everything.

"I'm sorry, guys. I should have explained. Remember what the queen told us when she presented us with this beautiful snow globe?" asked Magdalena.

"Uh, nope. Do tell," barked Piper. He was beginning to feel a little testy, too.

"She reminded us that the snow globe was enchanted and that if we ever needed her, she was only a snow globe shake away," reminded Magdalena.

Gabriel instantly knew where Magdalena was going with this, and he was almost excited.

"Yes, Mags! You are on to something, I can feel it. We just assumed the snow globe opened a portal that would allow us to travel back and forth between Lily Brooke and Lindtzl Kingdom. We never thought about it being an enchanted symbol!" exclaimed Gabriel.

Well, that turned the light bulbs on, and you could see each MALB member's face begin to light up as they realized they were holding the key to finding the queen in their very hands.

"Mags, you are a genius!" shouted Hubert. Before he even thought about what he was doing, he let his hand fall off the snow globe and flew his arms around her neck, giving her the biggest bear hug he could offer.

Magdalena gave a little giggle, knowing Hubert was really at his wit's end with all this evil stuff, and said, "It wasn't me, Hubert. It was the queen! She is the genius. We just had to realize what her Christmas gift really meant. She told us the globe represented our joyful time together, reminding us of the comradery we all share. I just got to thinking that since we are all here together in the enchanted kingdom, that maybe the snow globe played a bigger part of the puzzle."

"Shall we see what happens then?" inquired Magdalena.

All heads shook a confirmation, yes, and Hubert replaced his hand on top of the globe. In unison, they all held their gaze on the inside of the snow globe.

Before their eyes, they watched the scene and their last moments in the winter wonderland right before going home for Christmas last month. They were reminded of the joyous occasion after defeating the demonic curse of the werewolf gatekeepers. Little Skully had been such a fierce and evil animal.

Magdalena looked down at Skully, who seemed to watch and understand the scene that played out inside of the snow globe. *Look at him now,* thought Magdalena. Such a sweet and loyal soul. Remove the evil curse, and the three-headed werewolf had become the queen's most loyal patron. Why Skully had traveled through the hidden vortex all on his own and found Magdalena. It had to be a scary excursion.

As her eyes moved back to the snow globe scene, she realized what she needed to do.

"Everyone, please, drop your hands for just a moment," said Magdalena.

All hands dropped from the globe, and Magdalena gave it a gentle shake. The queen had said she was just a snow globe shake away.

As the snow inside of the globe began to fall, Magdalena chanted, "Snow globe, snow globe, winter and all, bring forth our queen, let her know we are here, one and all."

Magdalena held out the snow globe in the middle of the circle once again, and the friends instinctively knew to place their hands back on the globe.

As all eyes were watching the snowfall inside of the globe while the children were enjoying the Christmas feast, dark clouds began to close in on the group.

It took a moment for MALB to realize the dark clouds, and the ominous sky was not only happening inside of the globe, but it was also happening live where they were standing in The Enchanted Forest.

"Woah, guys! Whatever is happening inside of the globe is also happening here!" screeched Hubert. He was full-on terrified now. "The last time I saw clouds and a sky that looked like this was when the demons were mad and coming for us!"

Hubert had a point.

"Keep your eyes on the globe," reminded Magdalena. "This is the only way we can find the queen, no matter what happens around us. We are lost without her clue!"

The gang continued to watch the scene inside of the globe while each one of them secretly prayed it had nothing to do with demons.

Suddenly the dark clouds inside of the globe dispersed, and Queen Lindtzl appeared. She looked very sickly and worn. She didn't look anything like the beautiful queen they had met in December. Cody almost wasn't sure it was the same queen.

"Queen Lindtzl!" shouted Magdalena. "Where are you? What is happening? We can't get inside the castle. The door to tunnel number two is locked, and we can't get in from The Enchanted Forest!"

Piper began scanning the area around them, wondering if the queen was really near them since what was happening inside of the globe seemed to be happening outside of the globe.

"My dears! So good of you to come. I'm so thankful Skully made it to you. I trust you read my letter. We will discuss it more when I see you. I have been captured."

"Are you in the dungeon, queen?" asked Greta.

"No. I am being held in a secret underground mine. It's a long story, but I'm going to try to tell it as fast as I can in case we get cut off. The magic inside of the globe will only work so long with each shake," said the queen.

"We are listening," whispered Magdalena.

Everyone leaned in closer as the queen's words were soft-spoken, and they could tell she was quite weak.

"After you returned home for Christmas, I had some of the best days of my life since I lost my king. I moved back into the castle, and order was restored to Lindtzl Kingdom. I will eternally be grateful for your help in defeating the werewolf curse," smiled the queen. After a few deep breaths, she continued.

"Not long after everything seemed to be back in order, there was a knock at the front castle door. It was a cold, snowy day and almost blizzard conditions. I answered the door, and a homeless looking peddler begged for shelter from the storm. Not feeling threatened in any way, I invited him inside of the castle door. Once the peddler stepped over the threshold, his appearance quickly changed."

Hubert wasn't sure where this was going, but suddenly words like black magic, enchanted symbols, demons, werewolves, and spells started spinning around in his mind. He REALLY didn't like where this could be going. Not to mention, he was freezing in the now evil looking winter wonderland.

"Queen, what happened?" pushed Gabriel.

"It was old magic, Gabriel. I was too trusting. It's my fault," cried the queen.

"No, it wasn't your fault. You were kind, and good will always trump evil, queen. Never forget that," stated Magdalena.

She felt anger well up within her that was about to come spewing out in a vicious storm when she figured out who had captured the queen in her own home from what was meant to be an act of kindness.

The queen nodded acceptance of Magdalena's words and continued.

"Within a few seconds, the peddler's appearance changed in a dust storm of purple haze. Left standing in front of me was an evil troll. The troll had used old-style black magic to change his appearance. This type of magic only works if you are invited into the home. In other words, if the troll had entered the castle un-invited, the magic wouldn't have worked," explained the queen.

"So, what happened next?" asked Piper.

"Once I was face to face with the troll, I knew I was in trouble as I had invited him inside. My powers would not work against the curse. My enchanted abilities have been diminished, and I have become feeble and weak. I get weaker by the hour and am beginning to get sick. If the curse isn't broken soon, I'm afraid I won't make it, my friends."

Magdalena couldn't believe her own ears. How could this have happened, and so soon since the queen had taken back control of the kingdom?

"What does the troll want? Why are you being held captive? All of this because he wants to rule the kingdom, or what?" asked Cody.

MALB was not prepared for what came next. As a matter of fact, Magdalena wasn't sure how to react.

UNDERGROUND MINE
~ Seven ~

"I'm afraid it is greed and not power this time, Cody," replied the queen. "The troll had learned about the hidden mine in Lindtzl Kingdom. It has been a secret for years, and very few people still knew of its existence. Basically, it is a hidden gold and precious gems mine located in the depths of the kingdom."

"Those things really exist?" asked Hubert before he even thought about the question.

"Yes, they really exist but have been a coveted secret for many years. Only a very select few know of its existence, which is why I didn't expect the old magic curse," replied Queen Lindtzl.

"Why would they capture you, though? Why not just find the mine and steal the riches instead of holding you captive?" asked Gabriel.

He didn't understand the logic of the troll. If the queen didn't suspect anything sinister, wouldn't it have made more sense to find the mine, rob it, and leave undetected? Kidnapping the queen of the kingdom seemed to be much more of a problem than a covert thief operation.

"Gabriel, that's just it. The mine has always been such a hidden secret because it can only be accessed from inside of the castle. The troll knew the only way to gain access to the treasure was through the castle," said the queen. "I should have known better."

As the queen's words began to settle on the group, they realized they were up against a very smart and evil operation that had taken planning and precision to pull off.

Now what? Thought Magdalena.

Gabriel could see the queen was deteriorating quickly, so he wanted to get as much information as he could about how to find the mine. The castle was such a booby-trapped entrapment that he didn't want to have to explore every nook and cranny inside.

"Queen, how do we access the mine from inside of the castle? Right now, we haven't been able to get access inside of the building, but when we do, how do we find the mine?" inquired Gabriel.

Gabriel could see the queen was struggling with the information she had to present.

Hubert knew this wasn't going to be good news. Not at ALL.

Magdalena was praying it wasn't in one of the sabotaged dungeon tunnels.

Piper and Cody were doing that thing again, where they looked at each other and held a complete conversation with body language alone.

Greta was staring at the snow globe, wondering why she had stopped at Adolphe's bakery on her way home earlier today. If she hadn't of been there, Magdalena wouldn't have found her and maybe, just maybe, she would be home tucked into the warm covers of her bed instead of standing in the middle of an enchanted evil kingdom, hiding from evil trolls trying to steal all the riches in the land. Great.

"I'm sorry, guys. I am truly sorry to be the one to tell you this. In the letter I wrote to you, I mentioned to bring all the resources you could find. You will need them. The entrance to the underground mine is found at the bottom of the well in tunnel number four," explained the queen.

"No! Absolutely NOT!" cried Hubert. "There is an evil tree in that tunnel that tried to squeeze me to death. I'm never entering that tunnel again, riches or no riches. Sorry queen!"

"I understand your fear, Hubert. But you are my only hope. I don't care about the riches for myself. But that is the only way I can provide for the kingdom. If the trolls remove the gold and gems from the mine, they take away my power to keep the people of Lindtzl Kingdom safe," begged the queen. "I'm afraid I don't have much time left. I am being held in a room somewhere in the mine. It's completely dark except for the light of a small lantern overhead. I can hear them working day and night, and the only time I see anyone is when they bring food to my quarters. I'm not going to be any help to you. Keep the snow globe in case you need me, but I'm not sure if it will work underneath in the depths of the castle. It has never been tested. Good luck, my friends. My life is in your hands, yet again."

Magdalena knew the task at hand was not only very risky but that MALB would be dealing with a completely new set of circumstances. Just when she thought she was beginning to understand the demons, a curveball appeared. She knew absolutely nothing about trolls.

"Queen, please wait!" shouted Magdalena. "I don't know anything about trolls. Is their magic similar to the demonic forces we have battled in the past?"

"My dear, yes, everything you need is already inside of you. Always remember that no matter what, good will always win in the long run over evil. You just reminded me of the same. Love, friendship, teamwork, and faith will get you through any trial you face in the presence of evil. The trolls use old magic, which can vary a little from the black magic used by the demonic forces. All you have to do is use the enchanted abilities you have been gifted from the one above," smiled Queen Lindtzl.

Before anyone could speak another word, the dark clouds inside of the snow globe cleared, the sky turned blue, and the winter wonderland scene from last month began to play again.

MALB looked around and noticed not only did the scene inside of the globe change, but so did their current surroundings. The skies had cleared, and the darkness had moved out, but the stench and broken winter wonderland remained the same.

"So, what do we do now?" asked Greta. "Any thoughts on how we break into a booby-trapped castle in this evil enchanted forest that is now controlled by trolls using old magic, whatever that is?"

Even Magdalena had no response.

Little Skully's tail had stopped wagging.

Everyone stood motionless.

Knowing the queen didn't have long, Magdalena felt the pressure to keep searching for an answer to the obvious question on all their minds.

After a few moments of no one speaking, no one offering any ideas, and everyone looking helpless, Gabriel spoke.

"Magdalena, relax, and think about the queen's words. You have everything inside of you that we need to figure this problem out. And we have each other. What is your gut saying to you?"

Magdalena paused a moment to let Gabriel's words sink in deep. He was right, and she knew it. Even if she couldn't put it into words just yet, her mind and body knew they would find a way. MALB had to restore the balance of good and evil in Lindtzl Kingdom, and right now, they were all the queen had.

"Okay, guys, the queen needs us, and we are no good sitting here licking our wounds. None of us asked for this little adventure, but you know what? None of us asked for the previous two adventures either. We need to put our heads together and figure this out soon before we lose the queen in the process. I don't know about y'all, but I do not want to live in Lindtzl Kingdom."

"Excuse me?" asked Hubert. "Did you say something about living in this forsaken forest? Nope. Not going to happen!"

"Exactly," replied Gabriel. "So, lets come up with a plan to get the heck out of here and let the queen rule the land. I much prefer Lily Brooke and its hidden demons to this mess."

"Lord help, amen!" added Greta.

It would have been a humorous moment except that as funny as it should have been was as serious as it was. Nothing was light-hearted, and nothing was funny. This was a real-world experience, not something the gang had read about in a pre-teen mystery book. Those days of naiveness were gone.

Then it hit her like a ton of bricks falling from the sky.

"I got it," said Magdalena. "We make witchy soup."

That was the one thing Hubert thought he was the least prepared for so far.

"Didn't you say that witchy soup had screaming witches inside of it, or something like that?" asked Hubert. "Uh, Mags, I don't think I can handle demonic spells with witches screaming at the same time we have to battle old magic dealing trolls."

And with that, the air seemed to be thick with fear.

WITCHLY SPELLS
~ Eight ~

Magdalena knew that to get everyone on board with her plan, she needed to explain her reasoning. Although it would be scary and feature plenty of unknown elements, it was their only option.

"Remember our trip down the well in tunnel number four?" she asked.

"Are you crazy, Mags? Do you seriously think we could ever forget that ride, even if we wanted to?" asked Hubert.

"I know, Hubert; me, too. I would love to forget. But stay with me. What did we find at the bottom of the well?"

"Nothing," replied Piper. "We had to use the lily root spell to fly back up to the top of the well to escape the tunnel."

"Exactly," said Magdalena. "Which is why our only option is to use the twisted shrooms spell and enter the well again."

"Mags, I am usually able to follow you, but I can't keep up this time. I don't understand," replied Gabriel.

"The point is we didn't see anything at the bottom of the well. Queen Lindtzl just told us the access to the mine was found in tunnel number four at the bottom of the well," she reasoned. "Therefore, we know the access point must be hidden, and we won't be able to see it in plain sight. There must be a hidden vortex that we can't detect without black magic."

And the light bulbs went off, as the rest of the friends began to follow Magdalena's logic.

"Okay, so we need to use the new spell to find the entrance of the vortex. But what if we find the vortex and follow it, but then can't get back out and are stuck in the mine with the trolls? We will be doomed forever in one of those hidden rooms where the queen is being held," exclaimed Hubert.

"Hubert, calm down. Let's take it one step at a time. Right now, we need to focus on getting inside," explained Cody.

"Mags lead the way. We are with you, just let us know what to do," stated Greta.

"First, we need to find the ingredients for the spell. We need wild mushrooms, lily root, hair from a horse, garlic, and witch or wizard saliva. We need to find a cast-iron cauldron to cook it up. Once we have all of that and a place to cook the soup, it has to simmer for an hour," reminded Magdalena.

"Do you still have Sugar Baby's locket of hair in your pocket?" asked Hubert.

"Yes, I do! So, we have one ingredient down and several to go. I also have some of the dried lily root in the locket around my neck. I should have enough to add to the soup as well as keep some aside in case we need it for something else," said Magdalena.

"Okay, guys, so we need to find some wild mushroom and garlic. Magdalena is a witch, so her saliva will work," stated Gabriel.

"Our only option is to begin exploring these enchanted woods. As much as I don't want to venture off this trail leading from the castle to the outdoor dining table, we have to find these ingredients," said Magdalena.

"Lead the way, we have your back," responded Piper. There was simply no other option.

The group made a single file line with Hubert taking up the back. He always liked to be the last in line as he called it his mental sanity. If something ever happened and they had to turn and run, well, he would be the first to escape.

Unbeknownst to him, everyone else in the gang knew and understood this secret philosophy. But they also knew this was the only way Hubert would survive the adventure, so they always went along with it but softly giggled.

Magdalena led the friends, and they began walking away from the castle further into the mysterious woods.

After what seemed like hours, they came across a series of rolling hills. Gabriel scanned the area and announced to the group that they appeared to be at the basin of a large mountain range.

"These hills appear to form a valley here at the basin of this large mountain range. Maybe in these fields, we can find what we need," explained Gabriel.

"This sure would be easier in the daylight," whimpered Hubert.

The crew scattered out, and within a few moments, they were able to find some mushrooms and garlic growing wild.

"Now, we need to find a cast-iron cauldron. Good luck finding that out here in the middle of nowhere," smirked Hubert.

"Wait, guys, is that a roofline over there?" pointed Magdalena. "I can't tell."

Everyone followed her gaze. Just above the top of the next knoll appeared to be a small roofline.

"There's only one way to find out," said Piper. "Let's go."

MALB cautiously walked towards the grassy knoll, and within a few moments, a little cottage appeared. Indeed, it was a small roofline that Magdalena had noticed tucked into the countryside.

"Good eye, Mags," said Gabriel. "How are we going to play this?"

Cody had been considering the option that this could be a lure. "Maybe we should send one of us to peek inside the cottage. The last thing we need is to all get captured if this is some type of a lure."

"Good point," reasoned Magdalena. "I can sneak closer with one of the flashlights. Once I peer inside, if all is well, I will signal you to come with the other flashlights."

"I don't want you to go alone," stated Gabriel.

"I will be fine. If it is a lure, at least I have black magic on my side. If you get captured, Gabriel, it becomes much more difficult."

Gabriel didn't like Magdalena's reasoning, but she did have a very valid point.

"Okay, we'll be watching. Please approach with caution and be careful. We have no idea what we are dealing with here," said Gabriel.

Magdalena took Gabriel's flashlight and tried to crouch low to the ground while using the rolling hills for cover. As she got closer to the little cottage, she could see a small light peering through the corner of the front window. Not knowing if anyone was inside, she put her back flat to the outer wall and peeped into the side crack of the window, hoping to see an empty room.

As she took a glance around the portion of the room she saw, it appeared to be a small one-room cottage. One corner of the room featured a small bed that couldn't have fit more than one small person. It seemed a little odd to her with how small it looked.

She also saw a small round table with two chairs tucked nicely underneath it and a tiny rocking chair sitting in front of a stone walk-in fireplace.

There was a roaring fire in the fireplace and behold a cast-iron cauldron simmering on the fire. She couldn't believe the view in front of her eyes.

Now, to get inside of the little cottage undetected.

Magdalena cautiously approached the front door and gave the little handle a slight turn. Just her luck, it was unlocked! She absolutely couldn't believe the good fortune. Or, the not so good fortune if this was a sabotage event.

The door slowly opened, and Magdalena quietly stepped inside. She stood in the little one-room cottage with her heart beating so fast she almost couldn't catch her breath. She quickly scanned the room from side to side, and no one appeared to be home.

Interesting, she thought. *Had someone left in a hurry?*

She casually walked over to the cauldron sitting on the fire and peered inside. There was nothing there, but what seemed to be boiling water.

She quickly crossed the cottage and took one step outside of the cottage door while waiving the flashlight as fast as she could to signal the others that it was okay to approach.

Within a few moments, the rest of MALB had arrived.

"Doesn't this feel a little staged to anyone else?" asked Greta after taking a little look around the cottage.

"Yeah, I don't like it either. But we don't have much of choice, so let's get this soup thingy moving along," replied Hubert.

He was right. The quicker Magdalena had the witchy soup ready, the quicker they could get the heck out of dodge.

"There appears to be already water boiling in the cauldron, so we may not have long before someone or something returns," added Magdalena.

The group hovered around the over-sized walk-in fireplace as the warmth from the fire was comforting after their long walk across the winter wonderland.

Magdalena added the wild mushrooms, a sliver of the dried lily root from her locket, a few pieces of Sugar Baby's hair from her jeans' pocket, some of the wild garlic they had discovered and began to stir the potion.

"Don't forget to spit in the soup!" cried Hubert. "I'm not going to be doomed because Magdalena forgot to spit in the soup."

Greta couldn't help it, Hubert's words hit her straight across the face, and she laughed almost hysterically.

Somehow, Hubert didn't see the humor in his words, but he went with it.

Magdalena leaned over the boiling mixture in the cauldron and thought, *here goes nothing.*

She spit inside of the soup, and once the saliva hit the mixture, it began to steam.

"Now we are cooking," stated Piper. "Does anyone have a watch? Aren't we supposed to time this for an hour?"

"I do," replied Cody. "I just set my alarm for one hour. Let's hope an hour in Lily Brooke is an hour in this enchanted place."

Good point, thought Magdalena.

But it was the best they could do.

"Now, we wait," she replied.

Exhausted from their trip, the gang decided it would be best to catch a little shut-eye before they had to go to battle in Lindtzl Castle.

Gabriel took one of the little chairs from around the table and lodged it underneath the front doorknob. If anyone came home, they were trapped inside of the one-room cottage anyway. At least this way, they would hear them coming through the door and awaken before being toast.

For fifty-five minutes, all of MALB slept soundly. Knowing that every adventure had typically been an all-nighter, they were wise to take advantage of every moment of rest they could get.

Right before Cody's watch alarm went off, he awakened kind of startled. He glanced around the little room but detected nothing that should have alerted him. He looked at his watch and saw there were four minutes to go. He turned the alarm off, knowing he would be awake for the next four minutes.

Then he saw it. He saw the doorknob try to turn. They were caught, and he knew it.

He quietly and quickly woke the others with the shush finger to his lips while pointing at the door.

They could hear someone frantically digging for keys and almost cursing at the jammed door. MALB had no option other than spread out and plaster themselves up against the outer walls of the room.

The only light shining throughout the cottage was coming from the fire underneath the cauldron. Maybe they could overcome whatever was coming through the door using the element of surprise. It was amazing how just by looking at each other, every MALB member knew and understood what the plan was to survive whatever stood on the other side of the door.

With about two minutes left to spare, the front door came flying open, and the tiny chair crashed to the ground. The wood splintered, and the chair legs came crashing down beneath the chair seat.

Standing in the doorway of the one-room cottage stood the ugliest looking troll Magdalena had ever seen. She couldn't have even dreamed anything uglier.

The troll quickly glanced around the room and didn't notice anything amiss. He was stunned and wasn't sure exactly what had happened to his chair.

Fast forward a moment later, and the witchy soup began to bubble a purple haze through the air. Suddenly the room was full of witches' screams. The troll covered his ears and ran over to the cauldron. As he gazed inside, he saw the purple haze witchy soup and instantly knew someone or something had not only broken into his cottage but was cooking up some black magic.

The troll turned to find a light to illuminate the cottage, and before it could process what happened, a burlap potato sack covered its head. The beast found itself belly down on the ground with the force of all the boys holding it down while Hubert bound the wrists and ankles with the rope he had brought on the excursion.

Once the troll had been secured, the boys sat the troll in the one standing chair facing away from the doorway.

Magdalena had found an old thermos in the cupboard and quickly filled it with the witchy soup. She drank one full ladle in case they needed the magic to help find the way back to Lindtzl Castle.

Greta stood, covering her ears as the witch screams coming out of the potion was almost deafening. For the life of her, she couldn't figure out how Magdalena possessed the bravery necessary to drink the soup.

There was a smoky purple hue throughout the room, and Hubert was ready to get out of there. No one spoke aloud as they didn't want the troll to hear them, in case he ever recognized their voices.

Gabriel motioned for everyone to exit the cottage. Once they were all safely outside of the cottage, Gabriel removed the burlap sack from the troll's head as he didn't want to suffocate him, just to subdue him.

The troll was furious and frantically crying out all sorts of unknown words but couldn't see Gabriel as he was standing directly behind him.

Gabriel exited the cottage and closed the door behind him. No one knew how long they had before the troll would be found and unbound or break free. But this was at least a head start to make their way back to Lindtzl Castle before their presence was discovered.

Once they were a safe distance away from the cottage, MALB stopped to catch their breath. The light of the full moon lit up the countryside like broad daylight.

After Magdalena was able to catch her breath, she pulled out the little black book and began flipping through the spells.

"What are you looking for, Mags?" asked Cody.

"I am trying to find something that may help us get inside the castle. At this point, we can't make an entry. Going through the front door is a no-go, and we can't get the door to tunnel number two open. I'm at a loss," responded Magdalena.

Why did she always have to bring up the obvious negative? Whined Hubert to himself.

All of this work so far, and they still couldn't get inside the dang castle.

"Wait, here it is," said Magdalena. "I thought I had seen it before, and yes, I was right!"

"What?" asked Hubert. Curiosity was killing him.

"There is a spell called Frezepic," explained Magdalena. "It is supposed to freeze anything it is directed to immediately. I am betting it is the same spell the queen used to freeze door number two in the dungeon."

"That would make sense," reasoned Greta. "But door number two is no longer frozen. It is somehow locked. So, how would freezing it help us get inside?"

"Just trust me, there is no time to explain," said Magdalena.

Everyone stood in silence as they knew Magdalena was memorizing the spell and obviously had a plan. At this point, it was the only plan they had, even if they didn't know the plan.

"Let's hurry," whispered Magdalena. "I want to get inside of the castle before someone discovers the troll, and our secret is out. Currently, we have the element of surprise, and I want to keep it that way."

MALB fell into the single-file line they often used as they all wanted to be sure to look from every angle while they were traipsing through The Enchanted Forest.

At least we are out of the open countryside, surmised Magdalena.

They were moving at a brisk pace, and before long, they had managed to return to the trail leading to the back door of the castle dungeon.

As they approached the door to tunnel number two, Magdalena entered her infamous trance-like state, and her eyes began glowing that familiar bold purple hue.

Hubert was scared and shaking in the knees.

LINDTZL CASTLE
~ Nine ~

MALB surrounded Magdalena and watched in awe as she cast the spell.

"Frezepic, Frezepic, you're no friend of mine, Frezepic, Frezepic, turn this door into frozen on the turn of a dime," chanted Magdalena.

With strong, forceful howling winds that came from nowhere, everyone but Magdalena landed square on their backs in the freezing snow.

Hubert threw his arms up over his eyes, trying to shield the blinding snow while Gabriel struggled to keep his eyes open to make sure nothing happened to his beloved Magdalena.

The circling gusts were too powerful for any of the MALB members to get back on their feet. Each one tried with all their might to keep eyes at all times on Magdalena to make sure she didn't disappear.

As quickly as the wind gusts had appeared, they were suddenly gone.

The gang scrambled to their feet, and Magdalena stood to face the door. She hadn't moved or flinched since she had entered the trance-like state to cast the spell.

Gabriel noticed the purple haze had evaporated, and Magdalena's stance seemed to relax. Within a few moments, she looked like Mags again.

Magdalena looked at the door in front of her, the one that led inside the castle down tunnel number two. It was completely frozen.

"Look! The door is now frozen," exclaimed Greta. "Now what? Shine the flashlight?"

"No. That will simply cause the ice to melt, and we will be right back to where we started," reminded Magdalena.

"Oh yeah, I guess you're right," whimpered Greta.

"Everyone, stand back," warned Magdalena. "You are about to see flying ice, and if you get hit, it will surely hurt."

Not wanting to take any chances, the friends found cover behind trees near the frozen door to protect them from whatever Magdalena planned to do next. Peeking around the tree trunks were inquisitive eyes.

Magdalena stood with her feet shoulder-width apart and began to focus all of her energy onto the frozen door facing. As her trance intensified, she began to slowly raise her arms until they were extended directly in front of her at shoulder level.

MALB didn't know what was about to happen, but they were very glad to be standing behind the evergreen trees. Lord only knew what Magdalena would do next.

Magdalena began rolling her fingers in a type of wave action like she was beckoning the door to open towards her. It was as though she was opening the door with mind control.

Suddenly, the door exploded into thousands of small ice chips that looked like bats frantically leaving a cave. Frozen pieces of ice were flying everywhere, and MALB was left covering their faces with their arms and ducking their heads into the base of the tree trunks.

Gabriel had seen nothing like this before. He had witnessed some shocking things since Magdalena had discovered her black magic abilities, but nothing on this scale. This was utterly unfathomable.

Once the flying ice seemed to stop, MALB carefully peered around their tree covers and stepped back onto the open path beside Magdalena.

As they noticed she was still staring at the door, they turned to face the massive opening leading into the tunnel where the door to tunnel number two had once been found. There was nothing left, and nothing preventing them from accessing the castle dungeon now.

"Oh my gosh, you did it, Mags!" cried out Hubert. He couldn't believe the openness in front of him.

"Wow, if I weren't already a believer, I sure would be now," stammered Piper.

"Are you okay, Mags?" asked Gabriel. He knew that every time Magdalena performed one of these high energy spells, it had the potential of leaving her weak.

Magdalena turned to her friends and said, "I will be fine. We need to hurry and get to the queen because I am sensing she is very weak."

"Lead the way," said Cody.

Magdalena led the group down tunnel number two and couldn't help the queasiness she felt in the pit of her stomach as they ran away from the winter wonderland.

Afraid to use too much light and alert anyone that could be on security patrol, Magdalena used the only flashlight at the head of the line. She was swinging the flashlight from side to side to see and potentially warn her friends of any hidden surprise attacks.

Much to her relief, nothing in the tunnels seemed suspicious.

As they reached the end of tunnel number two, they passed the long staircase of stone steps that led up through the bowels of the castle, eventually into the foyer. None of them would ever forget running up and down those stairs over and over while trying to escape the evil three-headed werewolf.

Speaking of werewolves, little Skully was still keeping up with the group. He was on Magdalena's heels, sniffing the ground on alert for any hidden trolls or demons along the way.

Mac was hiding underneath Cody's jacket with nothing but his little face popping through for air. Although Mac had matured some and would listen to light commands, the entire experience must have straightened him out a little as typically he wasn't that clingy type of a pup.

As Magdalena neared the entrance to tunnel number four, she thought she might be sick. Last time MALB had ventured down this tunnel through the dungeon door, they had held on for dear life.

On the other side of the door leading to dungeon number four, was a wicked and evil over-grown tree. It appeared harmless upon entrance to the dungeon. But when you least expected it, the tree would sweep you up off the ground and shake, squeeze, and swing its prey through the air.

Once it felt the prey was no longer a worthy opponent, it threw them through an opening in the floor that led to the bottom of a musty dried up well.

MALB reached the door to tunnel number four, and you could have heard a pin drop. No one in that tunnel wanted even to consider opening that door.

Hubert turned green again, yet no one could tell as they were in pure darkness other than Magdalena's lone flashlight.

"What's the plan, Mags?" asked Gabriel.

"I'm going to sing the tree to sleep again," she smiled. "No one moves an inch."

She didn't have to tell them twice. No one, even Skully nor Mac, breathed a hair. Nope. No one wanted an adventure with the wicked tree again.

Magdalena cracked the door open just enough for the air in the tunnel to filter into the dungeon room.

She grabbed her locket from underneath her sweatshirt and held onto the dried lily root inside of the necklace.

"Lily root, lily root, agent of the night, put this wicked tree to sleep by singing a soft lullaby. Let it only awake to the snap of my fingers, hear me now!" shouted Magdalena.

She waited patiently, crouched down to the floor in the tunnel hallway. She listened intently to see if she could detect any movement from the evil tree.

Not hearing a thing, she carefully opened the door further and touched one of the large roots that had popped through the concrete floor.

The tree didn't move.

Magdalena signaled to her friends with the shush finger sign to her lips to be quiet as she didn't want the tree to awaken.

One by one, they carefully entered the room as quietly as a mouse. Somehow, even Skully and Mac knew not to bark or make a sound.

As they reached the far side of the dungeon room, Magdalena saw the large round opening in the floor that was the mouth of the abandoned well. The friends instinctively surrounded the well opening holding hands, and Magdalena whispered a spell for each of them to fly safely to the ground of the well. Skully was wrapped around Magdalena's back for safe flight.

The group softly landed on the musty, damp floor of the dried-up well. Hubert didn't like feeling trapped, but at least this time, that darn tree had slept and not tried to kill him by making him human putty.

"Well, that went much better than last time," whispered Greta.

"Yeah, I agree," piped up Cody.

"Now the real fun begins," said Magdalena. "We need to figure out where the hidden vortex is so that we can enter the secret underground mine."

"How do we do that? We searched every stone in this well when we were trapped here last time and found nothing," asked Piper.

"This is where my witchy soup comes in to play," smiled Magdalena. "Remember, it helps to identify hidden vortexes and portals, which is why it was so important to cook it up in the little cottage."

For some reason, this puzzle piece just fell into place for quite a few of the MALB members. Even though they had followed Magdalena's logic all along, the gravity of the moment just clicked. Now they understood why she had been so intent on cooking her witchy soup.

"Ah, now I get it!" exclaimed Hubert.

If Magdalena wasn't mistaken, she thought Hubert almost sounded excited.

"Time to get drinking more of that purple witch screaming concoction, Magdalena," laughed Hubert.

Gabriel and Magdalena exchanged the all-knowing glance that let each other know that Hubert had now entered the next phase of fear, which was called delirium.

Magdalena just let him laugh for a few moments before he realized how exhausted he was and sat down on the floor beside Cody.

Pulling the thermos from her hoodie pocket, Magdalena opened the lid.

Out came a purple haze so thick that MALB almost couldn't see each other, and the screeches that entered the air were almost ear piercing.

"I certainly hope this doesn't wake up the evil tree upstairs," panted Piper.

"Well, if it does, we will have to deal with that on the way out of this forsaken place," retorted Hubert.

Magdalena closed her eyes, took a deep breath, and took a large gulp of the twisted shroom soup. She prayed that she had made the right decision. It was one thing to read about a spell in a little black book. It was something else to mix up black magic, cook it, and drink it. One never knew how the body would react to a large dose of a witch's spell.

In true fashion, Magdalena opened her eyes and could feel the potion begin to take hold of her senses. She now had tunnel vision. As she slowly turned around the bottom of the well, her friends' appearances became distorted. Instead of looking like humans, they looked more like pixels on television but with depth.

She tried to relax and not panic. Eventually, the spell would wear off, she knew. For the time being, she also knew her friends would keep her safe, and she needed to try and focus her visions into something meaningful, like finding a hidden way into the underground mine.

"What's happening, Magdalena?" asked Gabriel. "Are you doing okay? What do you see?"

Hearing Gabriel's voice was like a breath of fresh air for Magdalena. It seemed to help calm her insides just a little.

"I'm doing okay, but the sound of your voice is soothing. Nothing looks normal right now. Everything looks like a tv pixel, and I can't see shapes as much as I can see depth. It is very hard to describe."

"Just relax and let the potion do its thing," advised Gabriel. "We are here with you and won't let anything bad happen. Try to concentrate and look for an opening."

The longer Magdalena scanned the room, the more fine-tuned her vision became. It was like looking through a three-dimensional pair of binoculars. Once she became accustomed to the images, she began running her hands up and down the stone walls, looking for a latch, a revolving door, anything that could be a hidden entrance.

Then she saw it. The gem was hidden in plain sight. They would have never found it or even known it existed without the twisted shrooms spell. It was such a profound find that even Magdalena was in awe.

"I found it. I found our entrance to the hidden vortex that will lead us underneath this castle into the underground mine," she said matter-of-factly.

"Where?" asked Hubert. "I don't see anything."

Magdalena raised her hand and placed it on a moss-covered stone at eye level.

MALB watched her, and as they looked at the stone Magdalena was touching, it looked no different than any of the other stones scaling the well wall.

As Magdalena's fingers warmed the stone, it began to glow purple. She gently jiggled the stone, and it easily came out of the wall. To be sure, Magdalena leaned forward and peered behind the area where the stone had just been.

Behind the stone, well wall was a lantern hanging behind it that dimly lit the area. Magdalena knew she had found the opening.

No one spoke a word as Magdalena turned to face her friends. Her vision had normalized, and the potion seemed to wear off quickly.

"Behind this wall is the entrance to the underground mine. There is a hanging lit lantern just like the ones we found in the sacrificial cave in our first adventure back behind Hubert's barn. This must be it," she explained to her friends.

"What do we do now?" asked Cody.

"I think we should leave Mac and Skully here by the entrance, so if we don't return or anything happens, they can escape and find help. I don't know whom that help will be, but if we all enter this tunnel and something goes wrong, we will all be trapped," replied Magdalena.

"I agree," said Piper. "We need a contingency plan."

Magdalena leaned down to Skully and spoke softly face to face.

"I am counting on you to protect us. If we don't return within a few hours, find help. I don't know who you can ask, but you will know better than me. Keep an eye on Mac, he is a young puppy and just learning commands, but will be helpful to you in the event of an emergency," whispered Magdalena.

By the wag of Skully's tail, Magdalena knew he understood exactly what she was trying to convey.

Cody gently removed Mac from underneath his clothing and set the pup on the ground beside Skully.

"Mac, stay with Skully. Protect us from the evil that exists in this cave," ordered Cody.

Little Mac took one look at Cody and then one look at Skully. Magdalena thought she probably imagined it, but it seemed as though Mac knew exactly his purpose these next few hours.

Magdalena slid her hand back behind the opening created from the removed stone and felt the lever with her fingertips.

"Everyone move away from this wall," she warned.

With one tug of the lever, the stone wall began to rotate and open. There, in front of MALB, was a long windy dirt tunnel that was illuminated with a long series of candlelit lanterns. For as far as one could see, there was lantern after lantern, and they were exactly like the ones found in the cave entrance at the end of the crooked trail.

Magdalena took a deep breath and turned to face her friends.

"Ready? We have a queen to save."

"I guess I am as ready as I will ever be," surmised Hubert. "Do you think there are any hidden rooms with food in them? I'm really hungry."

If Hubert's gripe hadn't of been so expected, it might have been funny.

Everyone chose to ignore the question, and the rest of MALB stood to their feet.

Falling into their single-file line, Magdalena at the head of the line followed closely by Gabriel, then Cody, then Piper, then Greta, then Hubert as the caboose, they began the long windy dirt path that led to the bowels of the underground mine. Or, so they hoped.

HIDDEN GEMS
~ Ten ~

The irony wasn't lost on any of the six friends as they began the trek through the underground mine. The air was cool and damp, but at least the path was dimly lit so they could see their surroundings.

But that was the irony. The path was lit by candle lanterns all along the way. About every eighteen feet, there would be another lit lantern hanging from the side of the cave walls.

None of the children had anything against lanterns; it was just what they symbolized. The first adventure along the crooked trail had been scary enough, but when they figured out the demon figureheads had been locked up inside of the lanterns and escaped because the children had lit the lanterns, well, none of them would view lanterns the same ever again.

It seemed as though the gang had walked for miles, but Gabriel was fairly certain it had only been about a half-mile when they came upon a fork in the dirt path. Each fork led to a different tunnel.

As though the fork in the path wasn't eerie enough, the repeating lanterns stopped as well. The rest of the path was in complete darkness.

"Uh guys, what do y'all think of this?" asked Hubert. "We aren't seriously going to venture any further into this underground casket, are we?"

"Casket? What are you talking about, Hubert?" piped Greta.

"Well, it certainly feels like a casket to me! Here we are underneath the castle in the dirt, no light, and that we know of only one way in and one way out. Don't know about you, Greta, but if Skully and Mac don't hold their post and Magdalena's weird mushroom potion doesn't work, then we may not ever find the opening in the stone wall to get the heck out of here!"

Oh boy, thought Magdalena. *Here it goes. Hubert's nerves are shot.*

"Hubert, relax. Let's just take this one step at a time and not get ahead of ourselves," suggested Gabriel.

"Obviously, we have a problem here," said Cody. "The path completely splits, and there are no more lanterns. We are going to have to split up to find the queen before it is too late."

"Yeah, the only problem with that plan is we don't have a way to contact each other once we split. Even if we had thought to bring walkie-talkies, they probably wouldn't work down here with poor reception," surmised Piper.

"What do you suggest, Mags?" asked Gabriel.

Magdalena stood lost in thought for a few moments contemplating their options.

Ultimately, she realized that if they didn't split up, and they chose the path that didn't lead to the queen, they may not find her alive. So, she decided the best thing to do was split up because at least one of the teams would hopefully rescue the queen and get her to safe ground.

"As much as I don't want to split up, I think it is our only option. We can't afford to choose the wrong path, and we have no way of knowing which one to take," said Magdalena.

"I agree," added Gabriel. "Let's take a moment and explore the beginning of each tunnel and just see if we can find any additional clues as to where these tunnels may lead. We can guess that one of them leads to the gem mine. Maybe the other leads to the dungeon rooms like where the queen may be held."

The friends spread out and entered the tunnel to their right, first. They pulled the three flashlights they had brought with them and scoured the area fairly well.

"Look up there, guys," whispered Cody as he pointed to the top of the tunnel near the opening.

"What?" asked Hubert. "I don't see anything. What are you pointing to up there?"

"Come closer," said Cody. "There is an engraving in the stone, almost as though it is a street sign."

The gang moved closer in, and sure enough, engraved in the stone were the letters spelling FAME.

"Interesting," said Piper. "Why would the word fame be engraved in an underground tunnel below Lindtzl castle?"

"I'm not sure, but let's keep looking around, and maybe we will find something that gives us a hint," suggested Gabriel.

After a few more minutes of tunnel exploration, the children came up with nothing. It appeared as though the dirt path continued into a dark abyss. There were no lanterns, no light, nothing.

"Alright, not much here to see, so let's try the other tunnel," said Greta.

"Gabriel, shine your light on this tunnel entrance and just see if anything is engraved on this one," suggested Magdalena.

Gabriel shined the flashlight in about the same spot where they found the engraving in the right cave.

Sure enough, the letters spelling FORTUNE had been carved into the left cave.

"Someone sure has a sense of humor," laughed Hubert. "Are we to assume that the fortune cave leads to the treasure? Count me in!"

Everyone was a little tired of Hubert's nervous comedy and wished he would just relax a little, but it was still a little humorous.

"Wait, guys! Come over here," shouted Cody.

The friends moved further into the beginning of the left tunnel to see what Cody had discovered.

Cody was shining his flashlight on the ground, and as the friends moved in closer, they could see why he was so excited.

In front of MALB were train tracks.

"A train runs through this tunnel? How does it start here?" asked Greta. "This makes no sense."

Gabriel had already decided there was more to this tunnel than met the eye. He had moved further into the tunnel and off to the side of the cave wall.

"Yep! A minecart runs through this side of the cave tunnels. I'm guessing this train track probably goes all the way to the gem mine underneath the castle," admitted Gabriel.

"How do you know?" asked Piper.

"Come here, guys," said Gabriel. "There is an old abandoned-looking mine cart off the tracks hiding here in the corner."

MALB moved closer to Gabriel, and sure enough, the mine cart had been taken off the tracks and hidden in the far darkest corner of the entrance.

"Someone has been using this cart as a means to get back and forth through this tunnel," advised Piper.

Hubert was connecting the dots in his head and realized that whoever decided to venture down the left tunnel would probably have to ride in that cart and come face to face with whatever evil was down there.

"Guys, I volunteer to head down the FAME tunnel with whoever wants to go and try and find the queen," said Hubert.

All eyes turned to face Hubert. Everyone standing in that tunnel knew exactly why he had just volunteered for the other tunnel. But that was Hubert, and to know him was to love him.

Trying to help Hubert save face, Magdalena replied, "I think that is a great idea, Hubert. Let's figure out how we want to divide and conquer and get going."

"Shall we try the old way of dividing that we used to when we played Royals and Robbers as kids?" asked Piper.

"That's a great idea," said Magdalena. "Here we go."

Magdalena went down the line and assigned each person a number in sequential order. She was number one, Hubert was number two, etc...

"Okay, guys, even numbers follow the FAME tunnel; odd numbers follow the FORTUNE tunnel. Our goal is to find the queen and stop these trolls. Our meeting place will be back where Skully and Mac are waiting. If for some reason, you can't meet there or if it isn't safe, meet at the old dinner table in the winter wonderland where we shared our Christmas feast together," suggested Magdalena.

"Deal," said Hubert.

"Deal," said Cody.

And down the line, it went with everyone confirming they understood what was happening.

Magdalena, Cody, and Gabriel would be exploring the FORTUNE tunnel. Hubert, Piper, and Greta would be exploring the FAME tunnel.

Magdalena's group worked on getting the mine cart back onto the train tracks, and within a few moments, they were ready to go.

Everyone jumped inside of the cart, Gabriel and Magdalena began to crank the axle back and forth which generated the wheels turning and off they began.

Cody sat in the front of the cart with his flashlight on low to illuminate the train tracks so they could see what may be hiding up ahead.

Hubert and his group decided to use only one flashlight as well to illuminate the dirt walkway through the FAME tunnel. Piper was the lead and lit the way. Hubert and Greta spread out and began watching the sides of the tunnel for any surprises.

As Magdalena's group got further into the mine, they began passing several openings along the sides of the tunnel. A large boulder appeared to mark all of the offshoots creating mini tunnels.

"Great guys, what do we do?" asked Cody. "Do we stay on the main path, or do we duck inside of some of these little-branched tunnels to explore them?"

Magdalena wasn't sure what to do. On the one hand, the queen could be kept inside one of these diversions. On the other hand, instinct told her the queen was probably being held in the other tunnel away from where she suspected the gem mine would be found.

"Let's stay on the main path. I have to believe this cart is being used to get back and forth, and I think it will take us all the way to the gem mine," said Magdalena.

"Yes, I agree," confirmed Gabriel.

A few minutes further into the tunnel and the tracks stopped short with no warning. The friends had been pumping the axel and moving at quite a fast clip and didn't have time to stop. Before they knew it, the cart flew off the tracks, tipped, and threw them to the sides of the tunnel.

Lying flat on their backs, Gabriel shouted, "Are you guys okay?"

"I'm okay but didn't see that coming," replied Cody.

"I'm good, just a little stunned. Give me a minute," responded Magdalena.

Before anyone could make a move, the sound of running people could be heard from up ahead.

Without saying a word, Magdalena and Cody were by Gabriel's side, and all three of them hunched down, hiding in the far corner of the cave.

Realizing whomever or whatever was coming towards them knew something was amiss, Magdalena grabbed the boys by the hand and quickly backtracked to one of the offshoot tunnels marked by an oversized boulder.

The three children ducked back behind the boulder and entered the side cave tunnel.

As soon as they entered the off-shoot, they flattened themselves against the cave wall, hoping and praying that if anyone checked the opening, they wouldn't be detected.

Magdalena could hardly breathe as she heard what she now knew were trolls rapidly heading their way. She could hear they found the overturned mine cart and knew they had visitors.

The trolls had spread out and begun searching the tunnel.

Gabriel squeezed her hand, attempting to reassure her that everything was going to be okay, but she knew they were sitting ducks.

Before anyone could blink, a light began to shine on their hiding spot. A troll was standing at the entrance to the little tunnel. As his light shone, the friends could see that in front of them was a little hill lit up in red gems.

Magdalena caught her breath. They were rubies! They had found the gem mine and were currently hiding amongst a mine tunnel full of the most beautiful sparkling red rubies she had ever seen.

Gabriel dared to look over his shoulder to get a better view of the troll at the doorway. He stood there about three feet tall with a mining hat on his head that featured an automatic flashlight on the front of it.

The troll swept the mini tunnel from side to side but never completely entered the tunnel. This saved Magdalena and her friends as their backs were completely plastered against the wall of the door opening.

Satisfied that the ruby cave was empty, the hideous troll turned and left.

Magdalena could feel the energy drain from her body and thought she was going to collapse.

The three friends could hear the trolls sweeping all of the off-shoot tunnels, which Magdalena now assumed were individual gem mines. Not finding any imposters, the trolls gave up and retreated in the direction in which they had arrived.

Waiting for another five to ten minutes after the trolls had left to be sure they were in the clear, Gabriel finally broke the silence.

"That was about as close as I ever want to get to a troll," he whispered.

"Dude, I still can't breathe. I thought for sure we were goners. If that troll had of taken one step further into this mine, we would have been caught," said Cody.

"Well, at least we now know we are in the right place. There are more rubies in here than I ever thought possible. No wonder the trolls have kidnapped the queen to steal the loot," sighed Magdalena.

"Now, we need to come up with a plan on how to stop the trolls," said Gabriel. "Any thoughts, Mags?"

Hubert, Greta, and Piper thought for sure they were on an endless path. It seemed they had been walking forever and the scenery hadn't changed one bit.

"Guys, this is pointless. Maybe we should turn around and head down the FORTUNE tunnel to back up the others. There isn't anything here in this tunnel," suggested Piper.

"Nothing here is a good thing," suggested Hubert. "The last thing we truly wanted was to see or face anything scary, evil, or wicked. Not today!"

"You may have a point," replied Greta. "We aren't going to find the queen if there isn't anything but a long dirt path down here."

The gang continued to walk a little further, and sure enough up ahead, they could see large boulders on the sides of the tunnel walls.

"Do you see what I see?" asked Piper. "Remember the sacrificial cave we found along the crooked trail in our first adventure? These boulders remind me of those. Maybe something is hiding behind these large rocks."

"We don't have Magdalena to move these rocks, though," said Hubert. "How can we get behind them?

"Good point," muttered Piper. "We don't have a witch or wizard to help us. What will we do?"

"Let's get closer and just see if we can find a hidden lever or handle or something that could help us out," suggested Greta.

The three children split up and began looking around the boulders. There were about eight of them total, about twenty feet apart, four on each side of the tunnel path.

They scoured each boulder area, but the entrances to the off-shoot mini tunnels were completely sealed.

"This is helpless," whispered Hubert. "Maybe nothing is behind these boulders, but we will never know."

"Let's try this last one down here on the right anyway," said Greta. "Maybe, we will get lucky or something."

Hubert rolled his eyes, but no one could see him in the dark. What did one more boulder change if they couldn't move them or see behind them? He knew this was just the biggest waste of time that had ever been.

As they got closer to the last boulder, Greta spotted something on the ground near the large rock.

"Hey Piper, shine the flashlight right on the ground by the boulder," stated Greta.

As Piper shined the light, the three friends squatted down to see what lay on the floor.

Greta picked up a sliver of white fabric. It was soft, smooth, and elegant. She smelled the fabric to see if she could detect anything and instantly knew it was Queen Lindtzl's.

"Guys, this is a torn piece of the queen's dress!" exclaimed Greta. "I remember this fabric from her gorgeous dress when we met her in December."

"She must be behind this boulder!" exclaimed Piper. "We did it! We found the queen!"

In both of their excitement, neither one realized the obvious.

"Um guys, when you are done celebrating, we have one more problem to solve," mentioned Hubert. "We can't move the boulder."

Boom. The realization hit Greta and Piper like a ton of bricks.

"Oh no, we can't come this far and lose her!" shouted Greta in desperation. "She will suffocate. There can't be much oxygen this far into the underground mine."

Tears started to roll down Greta's face, and there was one thing that Hubert just could not take, and that was a friend in need.

Hubert hugged Greta and did everything he could to console her.

"Okay, guys, you know I'm the scaredy-cat of the group, but even I know we have to do this. Any ideas on how to move this boulder?" asked Hubert.

"Let's all three give it everything we got and push on the count of three," suggested Greta.

The three huddled together, and on the count of three, they pushed and pulled and grunted and fell to the ground, pushing so hard.

The boulder didn't move.

Greta was crying again, and Piper had given up. His body language screamed defeat.

Hubert found himself in an awkward situation. He had zero ideas and was now desperate. Without Magdalena, no one had any black magic skills or spells or potions up their sleeves. He felt completely powerless.

Then it hit her. Greta knew what needed to be done.

She whispered to Piper. He nodded his head in agreement, and they both looked at Hubert.

Realizing both of his friends were giving him that evil eye stare, he said, "What? What did I do?"

Greta and Piper exchanged glances, and Greta took a deep breath.

"Hubert, I need you to sit down, please. I want to talk to you, and I need you to promise me you will listen to everything I have to say before you say no."

"If you know I will say no, then why are you asking?" inquired Hubert in his almost irksome kind of jovial way.

"Because we are now desperate and have no options," responded Greta.

Hubert could still see the tear stains down the side of Greta's face in the glow from Piper's flashlight. Knowing better, he agreed to listen as seeing his friends in pain wasn't going to happen on his watch.

"You know how Magdalena is always telling us that having faith in ourselves is one of the most important things in life? And that if you work together as a team, you can accomplish anything you need or want in life?" asked Greta.

Uh oh, thought Hubert. *This can't be going somewhere I want to go.*

"Magdalena knows that good will always trump evil and that when you put your faith in a higher power, God will give you the strength you need to battle all evil. The key is you just have to believe. You have to believe you have the strength inside of you to make something happen, and you have to be thankful for the chance you have to make a difference," continued Greta.

"Sometimes, when we experience something new or something difficult, it is easier to say we can't do it and walk away than it is to face the challenge and accept our abilities and limitations. But, with faith and teamwork, those limitations can be moved."

"Greta, what is it that you want me to do? What is it that you think I have the ability to do, but that I don't believe in myself enough to do it?" whispered Hubert.

Obviously, Greta wanted him to try something that she felt he could do to save the queen, but she was scared to ask because she knew he was the MALB resident chicken when it came to anything outside of his comfort box. But, didn't Greta understand that love would always trump his fears? Anxious to prove this, Hubert took her by the hands and addressed her.

"Greta, my friends, are my life, and there isn't anything I wouldn't do or at least try to do to save them from harm or anything evil. But I don't understand what it is that you think I can do but will be too scared to do," inquired Hubert.

"Hubert, you can move this boulder. And, you can do it all by yourself. Please save the queen. You can do this," replied Greta.

"Greta, that is the most ridiculous thing I have heard all day. I would love to move this boulder, but the three of us just tried to move it together, and the dang thing wouldn't even budge," said Hubert.

"Hubert, you are a wizard. You have denied it, and you haven't embraced it yet, and we all hoped you would be much older and ready to deal with the reality when the time came, but that time is now. We don't have a choice. You have to come to terms with this quickly before the queen suffocates," murmured Piper.

Hubert stood there, completely stunned. He was so shocked that, for the first time in his life, he actually had no response. After a few moments, he faced his friends.

"Why in the world do y'all think I am a wizard?" asked Hubert. "I always take up the back of the line because I'm so scared of anything evil, dark, demonic, you get the point. How do you think I am anything like Magdalena? She is brave, makes decisions on the turn of a dime, and is usually right."

"Hubert, man, I know this feels weird, but think about it. Your mother is a witch and your father a wizard. Now, I don't know how the lineage works when it comes to the *enchanted*, or the *chosen*, but I am willing to bet a pure human isn't born to two enchanted parents," explained Piper. "And, you shouldn't compare yourself to Magdalena. We are all very different from each other, and God gives us different strengths and weaknesses. But the one thing we all share is the strength found within."

As if the thunderclouds hadn't already started to roll in Hubert's head, they were now pounding. He couldn't hear, couldn't see, couldn't feel.

There was no way he was a wizard. That was for sure — end of story.

LEVANTE
~ Eleven ~

As Hubert's nerves began to calm just a little, he had to admit his friends had a valid point. It just wasn't something that he had admitted to himself.

Mrs. Mueller was a witch. Mr. Mueller was a wizard. Hubert had learned that a few months ago, he just hadn't taken the time to think about it or to process the news.

Maybe deep down inside, he knew he was a wizard, and that is why he didn't want to process the news.

But this led to the next issue, which was if he truly indeed was a wizard, he now needed to embrace it and try to save the queen. They were completely out of other options with no way to signal the others.

Greta and Piper knew in their hearts that Hubert would find a way to make peace with this new revelation because, above all else, Hubert loved them all. There was no way he would stand by and watch his friends fall if there was anything he felt he could do to help. And, it was this fact that had Greta and Piper hoping and praying Hubert would embrace it. Quickly.

"For argument's sake, let's assume you are right, and I am a wizard. I don't know any spells. I don't have any black magic skills. How can I move the boulder?" asked Hubert.

Boom. They had him where they wanted him.

Magdalena was right. She had told the others in secrecy that she suspected Hubert was a wizard and that he would be able to communicate with her telepathically. If they found themselves in trouble, convince Hubert he has the ability, and have him try to connect with her thoughts. It would work similarly to how Magdalena could hear the demons' voices along the crooked trail last autumn.

"Magdalena knows you have the ability," whispered Greta. "All you have to do now is reach her telepathically. Close your eyes, zone out, and concentrate on reaching out to her. She will help you navigate what to do about the boulders. Think about how she was able to move the boulders in the sacrificial cave last fall!"

Hubert was desperate to help his friends even though he wasn't very sure about all this. He figured he didn't have much to lose at this point, so he would give it everything he had.

"Okay, guys, let's do this. I can do this, for Mags," he replied.

Hubert stood facing the large boulder that was blocking the entrance to the mini cave. He closed his eyes and tried to focus on nothing but his breathing. He let all stress drain from his body and let his thoughts go to his favorite person from Lily Brooke. He began to envision Magdalena and silently call out her name in his head. It was as if his soul was calling out to her for help.

As Magdalena, Gabriel, and Cody were standing there at a loss trying to figure out their next step, Magdalena had a strange feeling come over her. She tried to shake it, but it only grew stronger.

"I am getting this feeling guys, that something is very wrong with the rest of MALB. I can't shake it. Someone is calling out to me," said Magdalena.

Then she realized it had to be Hubert. They must truly be in trouble. The information she had shared privately with Greta and Piper must have been needed.

She looked at Gabriel and Cody and explained, "It's Hubert. The rest of the gang is in trouble, and they need our help. I was right. Hubert is a wizard."

No one made a sound or moved as they knew Magdalena would need to concentrate.

She closed her eyes and began to focus on hearing Hubert's thoughts. She could see him standing in front of a large boulder in fear. She could see Greta and Piper standing close by. In Hubert's hand was a piece of white fabric, and Magdalena instantly knew it was from the queen's dress.

"They found the queen, but she is trapped! She is being held in one of these off-shoot tunnels with a large boulder blocking the entrance," shouted Magdalena.

"Oh, no!" shouted Cody. "Do something, Mags! Can you help them?"

Magdalena didn't respond to Cody but stood there focused. She knew what she needed to do. Removing the little black book from her pocket, Magdalena flipped the pages until she found the spell labeled Levante. She quickly read the spell and placed the book back in her pocket for safekeeping.

Magdalena was coming through loud and clear in Hubert's mind, and he was almost excited to hear her voice.

"I got her! I got her! It's Mags! I reached her!" he exclaimed.

Greta and Piper were literally jumping for joy as they knew they would now be in the home stretch to saving the queen.

"What did she say?" shouted Greta.

Hubert didn't respond as he was intensely listening to Magdalena's words very carefully.

Now that he had been able to communicate with her telepathically, he confirmed he was a wizard. On the one hand, he was almost glad. Now he could stop dreading it. On the other hand, he wasn't sure he was ready for the life that Magdalena lived.

It seemed as though something had taken over Hubert's body and mind. Greta and Piper had never seen him so confident. The tears began to roll down Greta's face again as she was experiencing so much friendship, companionship, teamwork, and love, even in that dire moment of the unknown. She was one blessed girl to have friends like MALB, and she knew it.

Hubert stepped in front of the boulder blocking the entrance to the mine tunnel. He placed his feet shoulder-width apart and slowly raised his hands and arms out in front of him with fingers spread.

As his hands slowly raised in front of his body, so did the boulder. It rose higher and higher in the air until it was hovering above the mini cave entrance.

With the boulder out of the way, Piper ran to the cave entrance and shone the flashlight into the interior.

There in the back of the cave, lying on the cold ground, was the queen.

"QUEEN! We found you! Are you okay?" shouted Piper.

The queen began to stir slightly but quickly recognized Greta and Piper, who were now leaning down by her side.

She quickly sat up and said, "Oh, children, I am forever grateful to you. You saved my life!"

Hugs went around the room, and it took a few seconds to realize that Hubert was still standing in the zoned-out stance with the rock hovering above the entrance.

"Queen, we have to go. Hubert is holding the boulder that blocked the entrance over his head, and we need to get you out of here before he loses strength," ushered Greta.

"I'm not sure I can walk," cried the queen.

Before anyone could blink, Piper had the queen in his arms and was carrying her through the mine.

Greta quickly followed, and once they were outside of the room, Hubert began to lower his arms slowly. The boulder was floating down slowly, following the guide of Hubert's arms.

Within another few moments, the boulder sat back in its original resting spot, blocking the entrance.

As quickly as Hubert had transformed, he was back to his old self.

Greta threw her arms around Hubert's neck and sobbed as hard as she could. He embraced her, knowing that he had just accomplished the most wonderful thing he had ever done in his life to date. And it felt good. Really good.

"Man, you saved the queen. All on your own, Hubert. I'm so proud of you," whimpered Piper. He was fighting hard to keep the tears from streaming down his face.

"No, it wasn't all me, guys. Magdalena guided me through it, and without the faith that she is always preaching, I wouldn't have been able to move that boulder," said Hubert about as humbly as Greta had ever heard him speak.

The queen was gaining strength in the tunnel as the oxygen levels were a little better than the small mine room.

"I need to get back to the castle to gather reinforcements to battle these trolls, or we will all be captured again," she explained.

"Skully and Mac, which is Cody's little beagle pup, are guarding the entrance to the underground mine at the bottom of the old well. If we retrace our steps, we can get back into the castle without the trolls knowing you have escaped. They will assume you are still locked inside of the mine with the boulder blocking the access," suggested Greta.

"That sounds like a good plan to me," responded the queen. "I think I can walk now. Let's go!"

With that, Hubert, Greta, Piper, and Queen Lindtzl began retracing their steps to the underground well. The queen knew the evil force the rest of MALB was about to meet if they made it all the way into where the gold was mined.

Along the way, the queen filled in the friends all she knew about the trolls and their evil plan to steal all the kingdom's wealth.

Queen Lindtzl knew how greedy the trolls were. They were so greedy that they had passed on mining the rubies, emeralds, opals, and sapphires from the little off-shoot mines. They were only focused on stealing pure gold, which would be found in the last mine in the center of the underground maze.

As the friends and the queen came to the end of the FAME tunnel, Greta couldn't resist asking the queen why this tunnel was called FAME.

"The FAME tunnel was built to hold prisoners that stole gems when they were mining," admitted the queen. "If you worked for the kingdom and were caught stealing from the kingdom, you were made famous by a public flogging. There would be a town gathering, and the thief would be held accountable to all the patrons in the kingdom, hence making them "famous." Once the public spectacle was over, they were jailed in the mini caves throughout the fame tunnel. Each room is just like the one where you found me."

"That makes more sense," replied Greta.

The idea of being imprisoned in the dark and musty tunnel would have curtailed any desire for her ever to steal a gem, she thought.

Magdalena could sense that Hubert and the rest of MALB had been successful. She opened her eyes and faced Gabriel and Cody with eyes as large as saucers.

"Did he do it? Did Hubert save the queen?" gasped Cody.

"Yes! She is going to be okay. They have left the tunnel and are on their way back to the castle to gather reinforcements. Hubert says the queen has warned there will be many trolls at the furthest mine down here, where all of the gold is held," explained Magdalena.

"What do we do in the interim?" asked Gabriel. "Do we proceed and try to approach the trolls or wait. I'm beginning to feel like a sitting duck."

Magdalena thought for a second, and then Gabriel saw that sly smile wrap from ear to ear.

Uh oh, he thought. *Here we go...*

"I think I have an idea," she replied.

MAGICAL DEW
~ Twelve ~

Gabriel and Cody stood looking at Magdalena, waiting to see what kind of a revelation she may have for overcoming the evil trolls.

"There is a spell in this little black book called Magical Dew," said Magdalena. "In theory, I can create a potion that travels through the air like a heavy dew that would go undetected in this musty underground mine. Once the trolls breathe in the potion, they will magically fall asleep. We can then over-take them once the queen brings in the reinforcements, capturing them all."

"This sounds kind of familiar," said Gabriel. "Have we used this spell before, Mags?"

"My mother used a very similar spell she developed when they created the black vaccines. She created a potion and had it travel through town disguised as dew droplets suspended in the air. Once the droplets reached the intended destination, they dissolved into the vaccine vials all the while going undetected," replied Magdalena.

"Oh, that's right," said Gabriel. "A little different, but similar premise."

"Yes. I assume she got the idea from this old book of spells," smiled Magdalena. "But the difference is magical dew will gently put the trolls to sleep. It is an enchanted type of sleep in which they will only awaken by the sound of my voice."

"Sounds like a plan to me," confirmed Cody. "How do we make this magical dew?"

"Well, that is a little bit of the dilemma," responded Magdalena.

"Somehow, I knew this sounded too easy," grumbled Cody.

"We need to find water. I can't perform the spell without water," informed Magdalena. "As dark and musty as this mine is, I expect water used to run through here somewhere. We know water used to be found in the well inside of tunnel number four."

"True!" agreed Gabriel. "Maybe if we spread out a little and feel the cave walls, we can detect an area of moisture."

The three friends looked and looked and couldn't determine any source of potential water in the immediate area.

"I think we are going to have to push further inside the tunnel to find water. There doesn't seem to be anything here," suggested Gabriel.

Everyone acknowledged Gabriel's thought process and began the journey deeper into the underground mine.

Magdalena prayed they wouldn't encounter another troll as they had back in the cottage before she had the opportunity to prepare the spell.

As they worked their way further into the tunnel, Gabriel noticed another slight fork in the pathway just up ahead.

"Hey guys, look over there. Another trail branches off from this main path and goes in the opposite direction."

As the gang moved closer to the area Gabriel had noticed, they realized just how narrow and thin the newfound trail was. It was barely wide enough for the children to squeeze through the opening.

"I'm not sure if we should follow this opening or not," said Magdalena. "I don't want to get stuck behind one of these cave walls."

"Yeah, I agree," suggested Cody.

"The only thing is guys, with how narrow and curved this opening is, it may suggest that water created this crevice and used to flow through here. Maybe we should follow it as I do not see many options," stated Gabriel.

Magdalena thought about the dilemma, and although she wasn't excited to squeeze through the hairpin crack in the cave wall, she did have to admit the importance of finding water was urgent.

"Unfortunately, I don't see much choice."

And with that last thought, Magdalena led the group through the thin and narrow opening.

Gabriel thought for sure he was going to be permanently squashed flat like a pancake. The passageway was narrow and dark. The only light was coming from the flashlight.

As the three friends wound their way through the crevice in the cave, they finally came to an opening. They stepped away from the cave and found themselves in a heavily wooded area.

"I think we are outside the underground mine and above ground again," said Gabriel, slightly confused.

"Woah, I think you're right," said Cody. "Look up!"

As they looked up, their gaze was met with the most crystal-clear sky and what seemed like millions of twinkling stars. The light of the full moon was bright and provided plenty of light for the friends to see each other without the help of the flashlight.

"I guess we now have a way to sneak back into the underground mine when we are ready, without having to go through the castle," suggested Magdalena.

"I'm not sure my body can handle getting squished again, though," laughed Cody. "Although, if some demon or werewolf or troll pops out, watch me run through that crevice."

Magdalena and Gabriel had to chuckle as although Cody was slightly kidding, all three of them would squeeze back through the tight opening to avoid any evil encounters.

The group began to explore the woods around them and began walking away from the cave area. The forest was thick in this section of The Enchanted Forest. They knew they needed to find more of a clearing in order to find a water source potentially, so they pushed on.

About fifteen minutes later, the dense forest came to a clearing. A moon-lit lake stood at the edge of the clearing, just glistening in the moon's reflection.

"Yes!" shouted Magdalena. This is exactly what we needed.

As Magdalena bent down to cast her spell for the magical dew, she could have sworn she heard a sinister laugh as a large net dropped from the sky.

Before the three friends could utter a sound, they were lying flat on the ground by the shimmering lake, covered in a thick rope netting. Trapped.

Realizing they were caught in a hunting trap, the children began to panic and pulled on the rope.

Magdalena could hear a rustling in the closest tree to where they lie by the lake and then heard a loud thud. A figure was walking closer and closer, and her heart began to beat much faster than it should have.

As the figure approached, she noticed it seemed very short in stature.

The stench was undeniable. It was a troll.

The hideous laughter was overwhelming to the three friends, and at this point, they all knew they were in the hands of a troll.

Magdalena tried to calm her nerves as she knew there was only one troll and three of them. Somehow, they just needed to be free of the trap long enough to subdue the evil creature. If they could capture the troll, she only needed a few minutes to create the magical dew.

The troll was almost over the top of the children, and Magdalena quickly let her friends know her plan. She just prayed it would work.

The troll reached the trap and seemed very pleased with his work. He was laughing and hoping to see the scared faces of his prey.

He seemed to be disappointed and disheartened that this prey appeared dead. They weren't moving, weren't panicking, didn't seem alive much less scared of him.

Well, this was no fun at all.

The troll stood there, scratching his head, trying to figure out what happened. It was just a rope net meant to distract and temporarily immobilize the intruders.

He began to try and figure out where to hide their bodies. The troll master would NOT be pleased if the imposters didn't receive a public flogging. This was no fun at all.

The dismayed troll sat down by the trap and buried his head in his arms while attempting to come up with an escape plan that wouldn't have him responsible for the three children's demise. He did not want to face the wrath of the troll master.

Magdalena was waiting for the perfect moment. As soon as she saw the troll hide his face, she jumped into action.

Her focus became intense, and the two boys saw her eyes turn purple. Scared to move a muscle, they lay perfectly still while playing dead.

Magdalena's gaze began to burn a hole in the woven rope netting. As the last thread snapped, the three jumped up without a second to spare and tackled the forlorn troll.

He never saw it coming. He was completely stunned and gave no fight. Before he realized he had been captured, the troll was face down on the ground with his hands and feet bound behind him. The rope netting that was meant to subdue the imposters was now wrapped around his own limbs.

Gabriel's hand covered the troll's mouth in case he got the urge to scream.

"Hurry up, Mags, I can't keep him quiet long," whispered Gabriel. "Get moving on that spell!"

Without another second delay, Magdalena ran to the edge of the lake, pulled out the black book, and began the spell. She spoke to the water, and Cody couldn't believe his eyes.

From the lake arose tiny droplets of water that had the appearance of a fine mist. It moved past Cody and slowly ventured to where Gabriel had the trapped troll.

In perfect timing, Gabriel removed his hand from covering the troll's mouth.

As the hideous creature opened wide to scream for help, he instantly fell asleep.

Gabriel knew the spell had worked because the troll became completely limp. No more struggle, no more fight to get free.

Satisfied they were temporarily now safe, Gabriel stood beside the sleeping beast.

"Mags, that is amazing! It worked!" exclaimed Cody. He was so impressed at the moment that he could have shouted at the moon.

"How did the dew make the troll fall asleep, but not us?" inquired Gabriel. "We are breathing the same air as the troll."

"Yes, we are. It's all in the spell. You have to be very specific as to who is the intended recipient of the dark potion," she replied. "The troll will sleep until I give the command for him to awaken."

"So, what happens now?" asked Cody. He noticed the magical dew was still hovering over the area.

"Now, we need to get back into the underground tunnels and find where the gold is being mined. There, we will find the evil trolls and stop them in their path," advised Magdalena. "Hopefully, Hubert and the others are back to the castle by now, and the queen is gathering reinforcements in case any of the trolls escape the spell."

Without a moment to lose, Magdalena, Gabriel, and Cody went to squish themselves like human pancakes while being followed by the magical dew droplets suspended in the air like marbles in the sky.

ROYAL REINFORCEMENTS
~ Thirteen ~

Hubert, Greta, Piper, and Queen Lindtzl arrived at the hidden underground mine entrance at the bottom of the well.

Skully and Mac greeted them with tails wagging and whimpers of joy.

If Greta didn't know any better, she would have sworn the ex-werewolf and puppy were counting the minutes alone while waiting on MALB to return. She had to admit, there was something very comforting about seeing them guarding the mine entrance, though.

Queen Lindtzl dropped down to hug Skully with all her might.

"Skully, my loyal best friend, you have saved my life by finding Magdalena and her friends. You were so brave."

Queen Lindtzl gave Skully a few more friendly pets, scratched little Mac behind the ears, and then waved everyone to huddle in close together.

In the blink of an eye, the entire crew was softly floating through the air as the queen gently lifted them through the musty well.

As the group landed at the top of the well, the queen noticed the wicked tree guarding the tunnel was still fast asleep. She had to suppress a grin as Magdalena had for sure been successful in entering the underground mine via this tunnel.

Everyone stealthily tiptoed over the tree roots, careful not to wake the wicked tree, and scrambled down tunnel number four heading to the stone steps that would lead them to the heart of the castle.

Nearing the steps, the queen took a quick diversion down tunnel number three. When she arrived at the end of the tunnel, she opened the rotating door to disclose the hidden conference room.

The nostalgia wasn't lost on the children as they remembered how this room was their savior during their trip to Lindtzl Kingdom last month. They had sat at the long table reading history books from the library shelves found within. They had built a fire in the stone fireplace that had been hearty enough to warm the room.

Greta grinned when she remembered Hubert had been so warm and toasty sitting at the table that he had fallen asleep. *Who falls asleep when they are trying to figure out how to escape a three-headed demonic werewolf?* She thought. *Hubert does.*

"Children, I am going to leave you here in the safety of this room. I will have one of my servants to bring you some food. In the meantime, build a fire and get warm. You will need your strength for the battle that is sure to come really soon," demanded the queen.

Hubert looked like he was going to cry extreme tears of joy. The queen was going to feed him, give him warmth, and let him rest. Amazing how these things meant more to him right now than the next best electronic gift on the market.

"You don't have to tell me twice, queen," said Hubert as he immediately went over to the fireplace to start the fire.

Greta and Piper rolled their eyes as they knew food would get Hubert moving quicker than standing in the path of an oncoming avalanche.

The queen quickly left, and within a few minutes, one of her closest servants had delivered quite the spread of food to the hidden conference room at the end of dungeon tunnel number three.

The gang ate as though they hadn't eaten in years. For once in her life, Greta saw Hubert get full. She couldn't believe her eyes, it really was possible.

Little Mac curled up in front of the fire and was sound asleep after devouring a silver bowl filled with boiled chicken and sliced apples. This was much better than the bag food that Cody tried to get him to eat at home. Life in the castle. Mac could get used to this.

While the children were resting and mentally preparing for what was next to come, the queen had sent messengers out into the kingdom to secretly call a town hall meeting at the top of the hour.

Skully was instrumental in helping everything go undetected by the trolls. Luckily, they were all so focused on mining gold; they didn't notice a thing.

At the top of the hour, the queen gathered the villagers in the back courtyard of the castle, so if any trolls happened to pass by the castle, they wouldn't see the town hall meeting.

"My loyal subjects, I regret to inform you that we are being robbed as we speak. I was captured and imprisoned by the evil trolls that have lived in this kingdom for years. They are greedy and determined to steal the treasure that provides for our kingdom daily. I have a plan to capture them and restore the kingdom balance, but I need your help."

The queen then lowered her voice and filled the townspeople in on her plan. Once she felt everyone understood, she dismissed them to prepare for battle.

Greta, Piper, Hubert, and Mac had all fallen asleep with full bellies by the warmth of the fire. They all jumped to attention as they heard the queen clear her voice.

"Sorry, queen, we fell asleep!" stammered Greta, and she shot straight up out of her chair.

"Don't worry my child, I was hoping you were able to get some rest," replied the queen. "We are ready for war. The townspeople are prepared, and the time has come to take back my kingdom."

"What is the plan?" asked Hubert.

The queen crossed the room and sat down at the head of the conference table. From underneath her cloak, she pulled out a snow globe just like the one she had gifted MALB. Inside of the globe was a replica of Lindtzl Castle.

Queen Lindtzl shook the globe, and it began to snow inside. Within a few moments, the snow began to clear, and the scene changed to the inside of the underground mine.

Inside of the globe were the trolls working hard at mining gold. They were digging and shoveling the earth, putting it in a sieve, and shaking it to find the gold nuggets. Once they identified the gold nuggets, they would throw them into a mine cart. When the mine carts became full, a troll would jump into the cart, and by pumping a hand axle, move the mine cart down a set of train tracks outside of the mine into a forest area.

"Oh, my gosh!" exclaimed Hubert. "They really are stealing all of the gold."

"I'm afraid so, Hubert. The exit to the underground mine is in an area of the forest where the trolls live. There is a large shimmery lake in the thickest part of the forest. The troll cottages are dispersed throughout that same area. There is a large watchtower in the center of their village. The stolen gold nuggets are being stored in large treasure chests that are kept in the top of the watchtower, so the gold is guarded at all times," explained the queen.

"If they are guarding the gold all the time, how are we going to get it back?" asked Piper.

"Leave that part to me," replied the queen. "For now, we need to communicate with Magdalena, so they know we are on our way."

The queen lifted the snow globe, shook it again, and within a few moments, she could see Magdalena, Gabriel, and Cody. They were just re-entering the underground mine from the thin crevice area they had found.

As the rest of MALB cleared the thin tunnel, they found themselves back in the underground mine tunnel. Before anyone could ask the obvious question of what now, Magdalena felt something in her hoodie pocket begin to shake.

Out of instinct, she threw her hand inside of the pocket and realized the movement was coming from the snow globe that the queen had gifted MALB.

She pulled the globe from her pocket and noticed beautiful white fluffy snow falling from the sky.

As the snow began to clear, she saw Hubert, Greta, Piper, and Queen Lindtzl gathered around the conference room at the end of the dungeon tunnel number three in Lindtzl castle.

"Queen! You made it back okay. I recognize the room, and it looks like everyone is there safe," said Magdalena.

"Yes, Magdalena, we are all okay, and that is the purpose of our communication. I have met with the townspeople, and reinforcements are on the way," replied the queen.

For the next few minutes, the queen filled Magdalena and friends in on the plan and everything that had transpired since she had been captured. She told them about the mine carts filled with gold, how they exited the mine, and where they were being stored.

"Wait, I know where that is, queen. We accidentally came across that same lake a little while ago," shared Magdalena.

She then proceeded to inform the queen and the rest of MALB in the conference room what they had discovered and their plan involving magical dew.

"The only thing that concerns me, queen, is we didn't see the troll cottages or the watchtower when we were by the lake," said Magdalena. "I don't know how we could have missed it."

"I wouldn't worry too much about that," said Queen Lindtzl. "The cottages are tucked back a little from the lake and are probably hidden well in that dense part of the forest. As for the watchtower, it will most definitely be disguised. Not to mention, you were almost immediately subdued by the troll and were in a hurry to escape."

The queen had a valid point, so Magdalena shrugged it off. They now had a plan, and she was certain it would work. All they needed to do now was find the gold mine and infect the trolls with magical dew while the queen and reinforcements surprised the trolls on the home front.

TROLLIFIC WAR
~ Fourteen ~

Magdalena ended the transmission with the queen and placed the snow globe back in her pocket for safekeeping.

Her hand grazed over the gemmed box keeping the golden leaf safe. So far, she had been fortunate enough not to encounter any demons and therefore hadn't needed to use the golden leaf. She prayed with everything inside of her that she wouldn't need to open that box and could place it back in her closet when she returned home.

Home. The thought of being home safe in her bed was almost overwhelming. Being in Lindtzl Kingdom had a way of reminding her how fortunate she was living in the small town of Lily Brooke.

Although she often spent time looking over her shoulder, wondering when the next demon would appear, she knew she was very blessed. She had a loving family and supportive friends. What more could one truly ask for? She knew no matter what obstacles life threw her way that her friends would be there to help and support her.

"Hey Mags, where are you?" whispered Gabriel. "Are you okay?"

Gabriel knew Magdalena's thoughts were miles away. He just wasn't sure if she had doubts about their mission or doubts about her abilities.

"I'm here, sorry guys. I was just thinking about how wonderful it would be to be sound asleep in my bed right now," she giggled.

"You mean you would rather be home, warm, tucked underneath the covers, counting sheep in your sleep than battling evil trolls in an enchanted kingdom?" laughed Gabriel.

Cody looked at both of them and wondered if they had lost their minds. He most definitely would rather be home than the current state of affairs, but he truly didn't see one ounce of humor in the situation.

Must be nerves, he thought.

"If y'all are done daydreaming, we have a few hundred trolls to capture," suggested Cody.

Magdalena and Gabriel looked at Cody and realized he was right. It was time to get busy.

The three friends picked back up where they had left off and begun following the FORTUNE tunnel into the depths of the mine.

Before long, they started to notice a dim light up ahead. Getting closer, they could hear voices.

Magdalena strained to make out what the voices were saying, then realized they were chanting. It was a deep, evil-sounding type of chanting, not some cute little song she was hearing.

Gabriel shuttered when he heard the chanting as it reminded him of seeing Hubert tied up as a human sacrifice above the bonfire in the sacrificial cave last fall. All had ended well, but it reminded him of the scene when they had battled the demons.

One look at Gabriel and Magdalena knew where his mind had gone. She too recognized the aura of her surroundings, and something about the chant brought back all of the bad memories from last autumn.

She shook it off, thinking she was silly — nothing here but evil trolls that were about to meet their queen.

The children inched up as close to the edge of the gold mine as they could get without stepping out into the open area. Magdalena looked over her shoulder to be sure the magical dew was still there.

Suspended in the air, the dew was still with the friends. She had to breathe a sigh of relief, as facing the trolls empty-handed may not go so well.

Before they could make a move, everything went pitch-black darkness. There was no movement, no light, no sounds, nothing. It was as though nothing existed from that moment forward.

The queen and the rest of MALB left the castle through what used to be the door at the end of tunnel number two. As they exited the castle dungeon, they followed the trail to the outdoor dining table where the children had enjoyed the feast last month.

It pained the queen to see her beautiful winter wonderland in such disarray. She had maintained such a beautiful home while living in The Enchanted Forest all these years. She couldn't understand how, within a few weeks, everything had decayed and turned so ugly.

Greta noticed the queen's anguish and placed a reassuring hand on her shoulder.

The queen smiled and wiped away a tear of sadness.

As the group made their way deep into the forest, Hubert noticed how dense the woods were becoming.

"We must be getting close, queen? The woods are getting thicker."

"Yes, Hubert, we are very close. Pay attention to your gut instincts. I know you have had a long day, and your spiritual hearing and awareness are brand new, but when it comes to the spirit world, your soul will know something is wrong way before your head ever will."

Hubert grimaced at remembering he had just found out today that he was a wizard. He already missed the simple life.

Skully was leading the group and stopped short.

Queen Lindtzl recognized this area of the forest and realized they were now on the edge of the forest. One step further, and they would enter the clearing near the shimmery lake.

She turned to the others and advised them to be on guard; they would now enter where the trolls lived.

Meanwhile, the citizens of Lindtzl Kingdom were busy making preparations according to the queen's orders. Before long, there would be several hundred trolls to deal with.

The queen, Hubert, Greta, Piper, Skully, and little Mac quietly and stealthily made their way to the watchtower. Once there, Skully and Mac stood guard at the base while the others climbed the tower.

Reaching the top of the tower, the queen cast a spell causing the troll-guard to fall asleep. As his body became limp, Hubert carried him down from the watchtower and hid him behind the bushes.

With part one of the plan complete, the queen led the group to where the mine carts would exit the underground mine. They would sabotage any trolls that came through the mine unphased by the magical dew.

Not knowing how long she had been out, Magdalena awoke with a burning sensation in the pit of her stomach. She couldn't see anything but instinctively knew something was very wrong. She couldn't move at all and heard nothing.

Gabriel and Cody both seemed to awaken about the same time as Magdalena. Gabriel instantly felt the knot on the back of his head and knew they had been captured. Cody still felt a little disoriented, but he knew they had been captured as well.

Gabriel's throat was very dry. After a few minutes, he realized he was gagged, which was why his throat felt like sandpaper. Luckily for him, the troll that had tied him up wasn't great at tying knots. He was able to move the gag from his mouth by opening and closing his jaw enough to cause it to come loose.

"Mags, Cody, can you hear me?"

Magdalena could hear Gabriel but couldn't talk. Something was blocking her mouth from speaking. The panic began to well up within her stomach, and she fought back the tears.

Cody fought and was also able to loosen the gag in his mouth.

"I'm here, Gabriel. I can't move, but I got the gag out of my mouth. Where are we?"

"I don't know, but obviously some evil troll must have come up behind us. The bad thing is they now know for sure there are imposters in the mine, and they will be on guard," replied Gabriel. "I almost have my hands free."

Gabriel kept working the knots back and forth, hoping since his gag wasn't that secure, neither would the binds around his wrists and ankles. A few more minutes, and Gabriel was free.

Gabriel quickly untied Cody, and they began to search for Magdalena in the dark.

Stumbling on her just a few feet away, they removed her gag and unbound her hands and feet.

"Mags, are you okay?" asked Gabriel.

"I have a knot on the back of my head and a sore throat, but otherwise, I think I am okay," she replied.

"They took our flashlights. I can't see anything. Where could we be? It's pitch-black in here," noted Cody.

Then it hit all three of them. They would never escape. The trolls must have locked them inside of one of the gem mines. Visions of Queen Lindtzl's captivity flashed through Magdalena's mind. She knew the reason it was so dark was that a large boulder would be blocking the entrance to their stone-cold prison.

"We are in a gem mine, thrown in here never to escape," she cried.

Magdalena felt the warmth of Gabriel's embrace. She was exhausted and feeling fresh out of ideas. Although she had been fortunate enough not to battle demons on this trip, these little trolls were sneaky and a force to be reckoned with.

As Magdalena stood still in Gabriel's embrace, she realized something about him was different. She couldn't put her finger on it, but she detected a change in Gabriel.

"Guys, what are we going to do? We have got to find a way out of here," mumbled Cody.

"Oh, no! Where is the magical dew?" cried Magdalena.

No one made a move. They had no plan. They had no weapons. They had no light. They had no hope.

A minecart full of gold nuggets exited the underground mine leading to the watchtower. Hubert, Greta, Piper, the Queen, and their four-legged backups were ready. No sooner had the mine train made the clearing, and it was off the tracks and hiding behind a large over-sized rock near the cave exit.

Before anyone knew it, the queen had cast a spell, and the troll that had been driving the cart was fast asleep.

"One down, how many to go?" whispered Greta to herself and others. "Wonder how this one wasn't affected by the magical dew."

This same scenario went on for about another thirty minutes. Time after time, the queen would put each troll to sleep, and they were accumulating quite the pile of gold-filled minecarts.

"Something is wrong," said Hubert. "I can feel it. Something is wrong with Magdalena and the others. These trolls should be asleep. I sense the others are in a dark lightless hole. Queen, I think they have been captured."

Queen Lindtzl froze as she processed Hubert's words. *He may be right,* she surmised. *I'm not feeling Magdalena's presence.*

"We have a problem," replied the queen. "I fear our friends have been captured and placed in the pit."

"What pit? You never mentioned a pit. Where is it?" asked Hubert. He could feel his temper began to rise. No one better mess with his Magdalena. This was NOT part of the plan.

"I forgot all about it until you said they were in a dark lightless hole. If they were in a gem mine, it would just be dark. You said they were in a hole. I forgot all about it! How could this happen?"

The queen was desperately wringing her hands and pacing. She was trying to come up with a contingency plan to save the children.

"Where is this hole?" asked Hubert. He wasn't sure he wanted to know the answer, and he had this sense that the queen was purposefully avoiding the question.

"I'm so sorry, Hubert. I'm so very sorry."

The queen was full-out pacing now and kept muttering how sorry she was over and over.

Greta felt sick, and Piper watched the scene unfold in front of his eyes, wondering if he would ever see his friends again.

Skully obviously knew what this meant as the ex-werewolf sat on its hind legs looking defeated. The tail was no longer wagging, and the sadness in his eyes was obvious.

"Someone better tell me where my friends are," raged Hubert. "We need to help them."

Queen Lindtzl stopped pacing and looked at the three children directly in the eye.

"Have you ever heard of a black hole?"

"A black hole? No," responded Hubert. "What is it? Do you mean a hole in the ground kind of like the musty well where there is nothing but just a hole in the ground?"

"No, Hubert. That I could fix. I mean a black hole," replied the queen.

Confused out of his mind, Hubert looked to his friends and saw they had no more clarity than him.

"A black hole randomly exists between your world and mine," explained the queen. "It is a void in the universe. Nothing can escape it, not even light. Everything that goes in never comes out. It defies the laws of nature in both your world and the enchanted world."

"Um okay, but you still haven't told me what it actually is," snapped Hubert.

"No one knows. It is simply defined as a void in space. Nothing exists there."

"Queen, I may not be the sharpest tool in the shed, but even I know for 'nothing' to exist is impossible," argued Hubert.

"On one hand, Hubert, you are correct. In your world, the laws of physics are quite concrete. Light is light, dark is dark, time is time, and everything follows the same set of rules. In the enchanted world, our laws of physics are very similar, except we understand that time and space can be bent. Therefore, our laws of physics may be altered from your world. Good and evil live much closer to each other in an enchanted world. And in a balanced kingdom, they reside peacefully. Lindtzl was one such kingdom for many years. It wasn't until the king was killed that it spun out of control. And when the trolls became greedy, well, you know that story. In a black hole, the physics are very different. They don't follow your world or mine. To this point in time, nothing known has ever escaped the entrapment of a black hole."

Piper had heard about all he could take. This was just completely unacceptable.

"How do you get into a black hole if nothing can escape it? This doesn't make any sense, queen!"

"The trolls must have heard the legend when they learned about the gold mine," replied the queen. "That has to be the case. The old wives' tale says that years ago, when the gold and gems were discovered in the underground mine, the king of the time had servants dig a hole so deep that it could never be escaped. Legend says, the king performed old dark magic and cursed the hole the servants dug, turning it into a black hole. It was an insurance policy that if someone decided to try and steal the treasure from the kingdom, they would be suspended in time forever, never escaping."

"How could you possibly forget to mention this minor detail?" barked Greta. "My friends may be stuck inside of this black hole and never knew it existed!"

"I'm so sorry! I was so weak for being in captivity for so long that I completely forgot about it. The trolls must know of its existence. They most likely captured our friends and chose to dispose of them inside of the black hole. This does mean, however, that the trolls know where the deep hole is," surmised the queen.

"Well, good to know the black hole exists, but I believe the most important thing now is to figure out how to save Magdalena, Gabriel, and Cody!" cried Piper.

"Yes, I would agree," whispered the queen. She felt utterly defeated.

EXTRACTION
~ Fifteen ~

While the queen stood trying to figure out how to save the children, Hubert was on to something. He had rationalized that his friends were most definitely inside of the black hole mentioned in the old wives' tale. This would honestly explain the lack of light and sense he had of them not being near. He also knew and understood that the laws of physics in Lily Brooke were much different from the laws of physics in The Enchanted Forest. For goodness sake, they had happened upon The Enchanted Forest in their last adventure by slipping on a puddle of water and flying through a hidden vortex. *Nothing normal about that,* he thought.

So, he rationalized that there could very well be a way for his friends to escape that was unknown to the queen because quite frankly, she was trying to solve the problem using the two sets of physics they understood. What if a black hole really existed, but its laws of physics were completely different than anything they had ever experienced? If that were the case, all he needed to do was figure those laws out to determine how to help his friends escape.

But Hubert had just learned today that he had any enchanted powers at all. He had no training, nothing. How was he to figure out the laws to a part of the universe that he had never studied, never encountered, and never seen?

There were some days that Hubert wished he never got out of bed. Some days he wished life was easy. Some days he wished everything in life was fair. While he stood there feeling sorry for himself, it dawned on him.

What would Magdalena do if the shoe were on the other foot? What would she do if he and not her were trapped inside of some dark and mysteriously lifeless hole?

Hubert realized all true revelations in life came through at the darkest and most humbling of times. It was almost as though one had to reach the lowest moments of their life to receive the greatest gifts of humanity.

It was in this most desperate of moments that Hubert knew the answer to saving his friends. He now truly possessed the one thing Magdalena had always tried to help him understand, but he had been too stubborn to grasp the lesson.

"Where are you, Hubert?" asked Greta. "You seem to be fixated on something else. We need to save our friends. What are we going to do?"

Hubert looked at Greta. She was full out sobbing now. He looked at Piper, and he was also full out sobbing. No one cared how they looked. Hubert looked at the queen. She looked like she had lost her best friend. He felt sorry for her as he knew she shouldered the weight of the mistake. And it was a mistake that could cost his friends their lives, but it was done in innocence.

"We are going to do exactly what Magdalena would do," replied Hubert. "Let's go. We need to get to that black hole."

With that, Hubert stood and led his confused friends to the thin crevice opening in the side of the underground cave. Luckily, he had paid attention to Magdalena as she had filled the queen in on how they stumbled upon the shimmery lake. Based on her description, it wasn't difficult to find the hidden access point.

With Hubert in the lead, everyone crawled through the narrow opening, which left no more than an inch of space to breathe. Winding through the crooked and narrow path, the friends found themselves back inside the underground mine tunnel.

"Okay, this is where Magdalena and the guys re-entered the cave. Somewhere between here and the gold mine further inside of this tunnel is where they were captured. Pay very close attention, and watch your back. When they were captured, they didn't see it coming, or one of them would have been able to escape," warned Hubert.

"What is the plan?" whispered Piper. "When we reach the end of this tunnel where the gold mine is sitting, how do we over-take the trolls? We can't try to rescue our friends with a few hundred trolls roaming around."

"Minus about fifty," added the queen. "We put at least that many to sleep and left them back behind the boulders at the cave exit. But that still leaves many more to apprehend."

Hubert leaned in and quietly explained his rescue plan. It was the only option they had to try and save Magdalena, Gabriel, and Cody from a dreary and dark eternity. It was also the only option he could come up with to save the queen's kingdom and all the townspeople that resided in harmony within Lindtzl Kingdom.

Everyone was now on the same page, and all senses were on high alert. The group moved slowly and cautiously towards the end of the tunnel.

Just as Hubert had hoped, he discovered the magical dew hovering over the spot where he figured his friends had been taken hostage. He knew the magical dew would only respond to Magdalena's voice and would be suspended in the air waiting. Now it was time to see if part one of Hubert's plan would work.

Standing underneath the magical dew, Hubert closed his eyes and settled his mind. He concentrated all of his body energy and tried to contact Magdalena. He needed her to know they were on their way and that he needed her help.

Standing in the dark with a sense of complete loss, Magdalena suddenly felt Hubert's presence.

"Hubert is here! We are not alone! Hubert, we are trapped inside a dark area. There is no light, we can't see, we can't find a way out," cried Magdalena.

Hubert could feel her cries, and it took everything he had inside of him to control his emotions and remain calm for his friends. He telepathically filled her in on his plan, informed her where they were, and that everything would be okay.

Magdalena understood everything she felt and heard from Hubert. But the situation was much direr than even she had suspected.

"Where is he? I don't see him. I don't see anything," said Cody.

"He was in my head," Magdalena explained. "His spiritual hearing is advancing. He knows where we are and is coming to save us."

She didn't have the heart to tell Gabriel and Cody the bad news that they may never get out of there alive. *Some things just needed to be kept to yourself,* she decided.

Knowing she would need all the strength she could muster, Magdalena sat down to wait for her friends to arrive. She thought battling the demons, and the three-headed werewolf was tough in the past adventures, but the task at hand seemed worse than anything they had or could ever encounter.

Each minute ticked slowly by in Magdalena's head as they awaited the arrival of their fate, whatever it may be.

Realizing that Hubert had been in the 'zone,' no one uttered a word. Once he seemed to relax, the group moved forward. What surprised Piper was the magical dew seemed to follow them closely behind. He didn't ask and quite frankly just didn't want to know how or why.

The gang knew they were nearing the end of the tunnel as there was a dim light ahead. The queen confirmed they were now on the threshold of the gold mine. This is where they would encounter the remainder of the evil gold-digging trolls.

The queen reminded them that in the center of the gold mine would be the black hole. If they mistakenly fell inside of the pit, there would be no escape for any of them. All would be lost — end of story.

Greta was shaking so hard from fear that she couldn't control her body. The queen felt awful but knew there was nothing she could do but support her comrades.

"Stay here, guys. I can't risk losing any of you, and I have to focus on Mags, Gabriel, and Cody. Your job is to stay put and hide against the side of these tunnel walls. I'm going to put the trolls to sleep with Magdalena's magical dew. Actually, she will put the trolls to sleep with my help. Once the potion takes action, you may then enter the gold mine and queen; please make sure they stay asleep. If they start to awaken, blast them with one of your spells," grinned Hubert.

The queen was so thankful to see Hubert relax a little. It told her he did have a plan, and this boosted her confidence that maybe, just maybe, they had a chance.

"I've got it, Hubert. Go save the others. These trolls are mine!" responded the queen.

Hubert closed his eyes and entered the trance-like state again.

Magdalena felt Hubert's presence and knew it was time to see what they could do.

"I'm going to be communicating with Hubert. I don't have time to explain, but I need you to do something for me," Magdalena whispered to her friends.

"What is it, Mags? What do you need from us?" asked Gabriel.

"I need you to believe. I need you to believe what I tell you, no matter what your brain thinks. And when I say believe, you have to believe it on a level that far surpasses any doubt your mind could ever create. It's called faith. I need you to have faith in me, faith in above, faith in His promise."

Gabriel and Cody didn't know what to say. Whatever was about to happen was going to be life-altering, and they knew it. The only thing was, both boys realized that whatever this was, it would either be a good kind of life change, or a really bad one.

"I believe, Mags. I believe in every ounce of my soul that you have this. You are the best person I know, the most honest and sincere person I have ever met. I trust you with my life. No matter what happens, I will embrace and believe what you ask of me," replied Gabriel.

Magdalena felt her body go limp. At that moment, she knew why Gabriel had seemed so off earlier that day. What to do with that information was another story, but now she understood. And yes, it DID make a difference for both of them. Things would be different between them.

"Mags, there is no one I would rather be trapped with, honestly. No matter what you tell me to do, to think, I will do it. I will do it whole-heartedly, I swear," promised Cody.

"I love you, guys. We got this. Do not move," Magdalena ordered.

She closed her eyes and opened communication with Hubert.

Using Hubert as a human vice, she mentally ordered the magical dew to enter the gold mine and subdue every troll in sight. She ordered them to swiftly fall asleep and not awaken until they heard the command in only her voice.

The queen, Piper, Greta, Skully, and little Mac, stood watching Hubert in the zone. Suddenly, the magical dew began to move from the edge of the tunnel and dissipate inside the gold mine.

The trolls didn't appear to notice a thing. They kept chanting that awful sound as the dew encompassed the mine shaft.

It took only seconds for the chanting to stop.

Hubert opened his eyes, and sure enough, every troll he could see was sound asleep. Trolls were lying in the tops of minecarts. Trolls were sleeping with shovels in their hands. Trolls were sleeping with their mouths wide open as if they had been chanting when they fell asleep.

It was a very awe-inspiring moment to see Magdalena's spell at work. He only regretted that she was unable to see her handy work first hand.

The rest of the gang couldn't believe what they saw. It was as though someone flipped a light switch, and all activity instantaneously froze. Even the queen was quite mesmerized by the scene unfolding in the gold mine.

"Okay, guys, go make sure those trolls don't move. Queen, this is your operation now. I have some friends to save," ordered Hubert.

Without another word, the queen led the others into the gold mine. They spread out around the mine so that they could watch all areas of the underground napping room.

Hubert took a deep breath and scanned the room for the black hole. He knew it would be a pit

M. Gail Grant

somewhere in the ground and knew it would be disguised. The last thing he needed was to accidentally fall inside of it, which would be the same thing as game over. Obviously, the trolls knew where to find the pit or Magdalena, Gabriel, and Cody wouldn't be prisoners to its curse.

As Hubert continued to scan the room, he saw the golden statue. He couldn't believe he didn't notice it before as it was quite a monstrosity. And, it sat directly in the center of the gold mine.

He wasn't sure exactly what the statue had to do with the black hole, but he knew it had to have something to do with it. If nothing else, maybe it was a landmark.

A stone wall created a maze-like design circling the golden statue. Hubert walked the perimeter so that he could see the statue from every angle.

Getting closer, Hubert felt the hair on his arms stand straight up. He recognized the hideous beast carved in pure gold. It wasn't an image he thought he would ever forget because the face had been burned in his memory forever.

The gold statue was a replica of the grand demon. It looked exactly like one of the demons MALB had battled standing outside of the hidden treehouse last fall.

He closed his eyes and could see the wind swirling around him and the gusts that kept turning into demonic faces, taunting the children as they had run to seek cover.

Why in the world would a fifteen-foot gold statue of a demon be found in the center of the gold mine underneath Lindtzl Castle? Hubert was at a loss. He needed to find this out before going any further, so he quickly found the queen.

"Queen, why is there a golden demon statue in the middle of this mine?" asked Hubert, completely stunned.

"Oh, Hubert, I probably should have mentioned that before. Remember when you visited me last time and I told you how before my king being killed, everyone in Lindtzl Kingdom lived together harmoniously? The demons, werewolves, witches, wizards, and general citizens all got along and followed the rules."

"Yes, I remember, but King Lindtzl and yourself ran the kingdom. Why would a demon have a statue in the underground mine?" questioned Hubert.

"Well Hubert, the grand demon was the gatekeeper of the gold mine. He was an asset to the kingdom by making sure no one stole from the kingdom's treasure. If you were caught stealing, you had to deal with him before your sentence," explained the queen.

"Interesting," replied Hubert. "What happened with the grand demon and the gold mine when the king was killed, and you were over-turned?" inquired Hubert.

"The grand demon was very angry and made life miserable for the miners. It was a slow escalation, but his anger and mood intensified right up until the night I lost my husband. It makes sense to me after Magdalena explained the grand demon's anger and resentment over falling in love with her mother, Leona, yet she married Paulos, Magdalena's father, instead of the grand demon. I think that was the final straw that made him snap."

"Somehow queen, I don't know if Magdalena will ever be free of the grand demon and his wicked ways. Don't get me wrong; he is living life inside of a lantern, but every which way we turn, there is some type of constant reminder of his vengeance," sighed Hubert.

"I never really thought about it that way, but you are probably correct," agreed the queen. "The grand demon was always full of greed. The kingdom thought he had the statue built to remind the miners who was boss and whom they would deal with if they chose to steal under his watch. But I always felt it was more greed and pride that caused the demon to have the statue built. He loved himself more than anyone else, and I think it was his reminder of how perfect he saw himself."

"That's it," shouted Hubert. "I know where the black hole is in this mine. It's underneath the statue."

The queen's eyebrows raised so high on her forehead they almost seemed to touch her hairline.

"You are a genius, Hubert! You have to be right. The grand demon built the statue so that he wouldn't forget or lose the exact location of the black hole!"

"This means the black hole really isn't a black hole. It means it is a normal pit hidden in plain sight. The reason it is "inescapable" is no one knows it exists or where to find it. It probably has nothing to do with physics, but simply old magic," explained Hubert.

"Maybe there is hope after all!" cried the queen. She couldn't help herself and gave Hubert the biggest hug before she realized what she had done.

She slowly stepped away, smoothed her dress, and cleared her throat.

"I will make sure the trolls do not interfere. Good luck!"

Hubert walked back over towards the statue. He examined it closely, trying to figure out where the hidden access point could be. He couldn't find anything at all that looked like a lever, handle, rotating door, anything that MALB had seen in this enchanted world.

He had to admit he was completely stumped. As he stood there staring at the statue marveling in how conceited the grand demon had to be to build a statue out of gold in his own image, he noticed a glistening in the eyeball of the statue.

That's odd, he thought.

Carefully moving closer, Hubert realized with the height of the statue, he would have to physically climb it to get close enough to the eyeball to see why it had a reflection.

Praying some trap door didn't open and devour him, Hubert scaled the façade of the massive statue. He was praying under his breath and wishing he had been at church earlier today as he could have used a little extra blessing.

Hubert reached the facial area of the statue and was able to lean his back against the nose area, providing stability. He reached up and touched the eyeball of the statue, and realized it was made from an emerald.

Wow, he thought. *I bet the grand demon mined the emerald from this underground mine for these eyeballs.*

As Hubert ran his hand across the front of the gem, the statue moved. He grabbed the nose and tried to brace himself the best he could and began to pray.

That's it, he thought. The eyeball gem is the key to finding the black hole pit. *Here goes nothing.*

Still bracing himself against the facial features in the golden statue, Hubert wiggled the emerald eyeball. Within a few moments, the gem popped out of the socket and landed in his right hand.

With his heart in his feet and trembling from head to foot, Hubert slid his hand in the opening, looking for any type of lever.

As he suspected, there was a handle right inside the socket. Knowing this would be his best or worst mistake ever, he pushed the lever down and held on for dear life.

The ground beneath him shook, and the gold statue began to split in half. The front side of the statue opened to the right while the backside of the statue didn't move. The entire statue opened up like a locket.

Almost afraid to open his eyes, Hubert peered around the opening near the statue's ear. There, inside, was a staircase that led to the floor. At the end of the staircase was a large open black hole.

Hubert climbed down the spiral stairs, one step at a time, careful to make sure he had his footing before taking the next step. He knew one wrong move, and he could fall into the dark unknown abyss. Although he had deduced the pit was most likely old black magic, he hadn't ruled out some enchanted, mysterious properties of the unknown just yet.

Reaching the ground, Hubert kneeled to get a better view of the open pit area. *It could be something like the musty well they had found at the bottom of the dungeon tunnel number four,* he thought. *Or, it could be an endless abyss.*

Meanwhile, Magdalena could feel tears of joy running down her face as they all felt the movement from up above. It was almost as though whatever contraption in which her, Gabriel, and Cody were being held had been blasted with dynamite. Everything had shaken hard.

Gabriel and Cody said nothing but were looking above them where the movement seemed to have taken place. No sounds, nothing to see, but something had definitely happened.

Hubert began to reach out to Magdalena telepathically to give her an update. He was a little confused and wasn't sure about the next move.

Magdalena immediately sensed that Hubert was very close now. She knew he was in much closer proximity.

"Guys, Hubert has found us, but he can't see us. That large earthquake type of movement we felt was

Hubert breaking into some statue. Apparently, we are being held in some type of underground pit inside of a golden statue of the grand demon himself," explained Magdalena.

"What a jerk," murmured Cody before he caught himself. "Who likes themselves enough to make a statue after themselves?"

Gabriel had to snicker. Even in the desperation of the moment, Cody had a good point. These demons were something else.

"Alright, guys, this is where things may get difficult. BELIEVE and have faith. We can do this. I think we are standing very near to Hubert, and I believe there is an old spell of dark magic that has been cast to keep us from being able to see the light or anything quite frankly," said Magdalena.

"What can we do, Mags?" asked Gabriel. "Do we just try to climb and feel for a staircase?"

"No! Do not move. If this is old black magic, we could be standing on the edge of a cliff. We can't see anything at all, so don't move an ounce."

"Then what are you going to do?" inquired Cody. All of this didn't make much sense to him. *How would they escape if they couldn't move?*

"When you have faith, there will be light. I have a plan, and it involves black magic. However, it will only work if you truly believe. Here we go."

Knowing she only had one option, Magdalena reached into her pocket and carefully pulled out the gemmed box containing the golden leaf. She could feel the edges and contour of the design as soon as she removed it from the box.

Closing her eyes, she began to focus and cast her spell, "Grand demon, grand demon, you are no friend of mine. Remove this hideous curse, remove it from this mine. You may live in darkness, yet I believe in the light. Your curse holds no power over those who embrace the light and believe you have no power."

Whatever the curse was that the grand demon had placed in that gold mine was coming down. The wrath was completely unmistakable. The ground shook, the walls shook, it looked and sounded like an avalanche inside of the underground mine.

Fearful for their lives, Magdalena grabbed hands with Gabriel and Cody and holding the golden leaf high above her head, she shouted to the heavens.

"Take us now, take us into the light. We believe the curse has been broken, evil has been defeated, the old magic has no hold upon the children of the light," screamed Magdalena as loud as she could.

Instantly, everything stopped. A bright white light appeared above, and the underground mine opened up to the heavens. The light of the full moon lit up the remnants of the mine like it was mid-day.

There was a staircase in front of Magdalena, and the boys and they began to climb it as fast as they could. As they reached the top of the steps, Hubert, Greta, Piper, the queen, Skully, and Mac were there to greet them.

"My child, you have beaten the darkness and brought in the light," smiled Queen Lindtzl. "You had it within you all along. With old dark magic, it only works if you believe you are trapped. The second you doubt the magic, you become free. The grand demon instilled such fear and doom in all who encountered him; they never felt there would ever be an option to escape."

Tears were streaming down all their faces as the children had learned a valuable lesson that day. Sometimes all it took was faith in yourself and others, and the will to survive, no matter how bleak the situation looked.

"I'm exhausted," panted Hubert. He had about enough of this black magic, soul searching, out of the darkness into the light stuff for today. And, that wasn't to mention the fact he now had to live with the fact he was a wizard. "I want to go home."

"Me too, Hubert, me too," whispered Greta.

After a few moments of hugging, laughing, crying, and a little bit of everything else, the queen brought everyone back to reality.

"Well, my dears, we still have a few hundred trolls asleep that we need to deal with," reminded the queen.

"What happens to them now?" asked Cody.

Before the queen could answer, the cavalry arrived. The townspeople had heard the commotion and knew it was time to act. They closed in on what was left of the underground mine and spread out.

The queen looked at Magdalena and said, "It is now time to wake the trolls. We will take them all into custody, and they will have their day in court."

Magdalena replaced the golden leaf into the gem box and placed it inside of her hoodie pocket for safekeeping.

She raised her hands and spoke for all to hear. "Sleeping trolls, you may now awaken and arise. Your queen's authority has been restored, and you are now prisoners of Lindtzl Kingdom, with your day in court."

As the trolls began waking up, they found themselves outnumbered. The townspeople had brought enough rope to bind the wrists of every troll. In a single-file line, the townspeople paraded the trolls out of the underground mine area and into The

Enchanted Forest. They walked past the troll village almost as if to taunt them of where they wouldn't be going for an awfully long time.

As they neared the castle, the trolls walked over the drawbridge and down the stone steps that led to the bowels of the castle dungeons.

The trolls descended the stairs and were ordered into tunnels number one and number four for safekeeping.

The queen made eye contact with MALB and said, "I have a few little surprises in the dungeon tunnels for our friends while we await the trial. One day I will have to share a few secrets."

MALB was too tired to care. They felt they had seen it all.

"Yes, queen, another day. I'm not so sure my mind can process anything more today," said Gabriel.

With that, all of MALB shook their heads in agreement as this had ended up being the longest night ever.

"My friends, I will be eternally grateful for all you have done. You not only saved my life, but you saved my kingdom. And, you saved us all from the black hole curse. No longer will my people live in fear. We will gather the treasure and hide it again in a safe and secure place. The grand demon golden statue will be no more. Once we complete the trial and restore peace to the land, we will have a grand ball to celebrate. And my dears, you will be my honored guests!"

"Oh, queen, that sounds like so much fun!" screamed Magdalena. *A grand ball,* she thought. *I've never been to a royal ball!*

"Does that mean we have to dress up?" grimaced Hubert.

The queen couldn't help but laugh. Hubert was back to his old self, and she was quite happy to see that he was.

"Of course, Hubert, you must dress up for a royal ball. Better yet, you will need a date," grinned the queen.

Hubert looked as though he was going to be sick. There wasn't a MALB member standing at the top of the stone castle steps that didn't have a good laugh.

"Till next time, queen?" asked Magdalena. "I will miss you, Skully. Come visit me at any time."

Magdalena reached down to pet the three-headed ex-werewolf one last time. Skully seemed to purr like a cat. He obviously adored Magdalena, and why shouldn't he? She had broken the curse and had freed him. Now he had the pleasure of living beside the queen in the comforts of the castle.

"Till next time, Magdalena. Be careful and enjoy your journey home," said Queen Lindtzl, and she bowed before the children before turning to descend the stone steps.

CONFESSIONS
~ Sixteen ~

The friends slowly walked back to the wooden dining table where they had eaten in the winter wonderland last December. It seemed to be the perfect spot to leave The Enchanted Forest and return home. It was here they had met the queen, it was where she had presented the snow globe gift, and it was there they had enjoyed the feast of a lifetime. It somehow just seemed appropriate to return to that special place before leaving Lindtzl Kingdom behind, again.

As they neared the table, everyone noticed how the area had changed. It was as though someone had waved a magic wand, and all the beauty of the land had been restored.

The evergreen trees were decorated with silver tinsel, white lights, and large snowflakes. It was a breathtaking sight to behold. It looked as beautiful as it had been when decorated for Christmas but much simpler and elegant.

"Wow, this is incredible! I'm not sure I want to leave here," said Greta. "It is truly a winter wonderland."

"I agree, it's amazing, but let's not get too carried away," joked Piper. "I'm ready to crawl in my own bed and get some shut-eye."

"There is no way I'm spending five more minutes in this place, so you just go ahead and pull that snow globe out, Mags, and get it ready to fire up. I'm outta here!" demanded Hubert.

Turning the corner, Magdalena gave a sly smile as she saw the wooden outdoor dining table up ahead. She knew Hubert was about to change his tune and quite drastically. She had to work hard to stifle a giggle.

Nearing the table, Hubert looked up and saw the most amazing scene before his eyes. He wanted to drop to the ground on his knees and worship the queen at that very moment.

Just like the last trip to Lindtzl Kingdom, the queen was sending them home in style. From one end of the dining table to the other was the most beautiful looking display of food that Hubert was quite sure he had ever seen.

There were meats galore, vegetable souffle, cornbread stuffing, cranberry sauce, pies, cakes, breads, and more food than all of MALB would ever be able to consume.

The friends sat and enjoyed every moment of their special dinner in the winter wonderland. Hubert had thought he would never feel hungry again after the feast in the conference room, but the battle with the trolls had left them all feeling famished. But most of all, they enjoyed the time with each other.

"You know, we really should spend more time together when we aren't solving some crazy demonic mystery," laughed Greta. "I kinda like Y'all."

"Ditto," answered Cody. "This is much more fun than running around trying to capture evil trolls and make witchy soup."

Everyone laughed and began to realize how sleepy they were.

"I'm ready to go home," said Hubert. "I've eaten so much; I don't think I will ever be hungry again. Well, at least, not before breakfast tomorrow morning."

Magdalena pulled the snow globe out of her pocket and gave it a big shake. They all placed one hand on top of the globe and closed their eyes. A few seconds later, they all stood in Hubert's barn. Sugar Baby was excited to see her best friends.

"Good night, Sugar Baby," whispered Magdalena.

"Mags, I can walk you home on my way," suggested Gabriel. He really wanted a few moments alone with her, and now was as good a time as any.

"That would be great, Gabriel, thanks," she replied.

Cody, little Mac, and Piper exited the barn and were going to walk Greta to her house on the way to their own homes. Hubert mumbled something that sounded like 'see you at school tomorrow' and stumbled through his front door.

Gabriel and Magdalena headed down Wildwood Lane towards Magdalena's house. They passed Rownalt Street, and a little light was still shining in the back of Adolphe's bakery.

As they turned the corner, Saint Irmgardis, their church, came into view. Magdalena and Gabriel had grown up together in that church, and it always held a special place in Gabriel's heart.

"Hey, Mags, want to walk through the rose garden back behind the church for a minute?"

"Tonight? In the dark and snow? What's up, Gabriel?"

Now he was feeling a little sheepish at the suggestion, but the truth was he wasn't ready to leave Magdalena tonight. There had been a few times he wondered if they were going to make it out of Lindtzl Kingdom alive.

"We can go another time if you're tired and want to get home. It was just a thought."

Magdalena knew Gabriel wanted to talk to her, but her brain was so fuzzy from everything that transacted this past evening, and she didn't want to say the wrong thing or mess anything up. She felt it was better to be clear-headed and focused when she sat down to discuss what she knew was on Gabriel's mind.

"Gabriel, I'm so tired I almost can't even function. How about another night?" she smiled.

"Of course, Mags. Let's get you home," he responded.

They walked in silence, and as they neared the little white picket fence gate, in true gentleman fashion, Gabriel opened the gate for Magdalena to pass through. He walked her all the way up to the front door.

She turned to face Gabriel to say goodnight and was met with a soft kiss. Surprised and startled, Magdalena took a small step backward. As she looked up at Gabriel, she could see the slight hurt in his eyes.

Knowing she wasn't going to get out of this moment without either confessing her feelings or hurting him, she walked towards him and placed her hands on his hands.

"You are my everything, Gabriel. You are my best friend, my shoulder to cry on, my everything. I know you feel the same. This is such a special moment, and I know I'm going to mess it up because I'm so exhausted; I can't even think. My heart beats for you. I can't imagine what life would be like without you. But most of all, I don't want to lose your friendship. And I'm afraid if I fall for you, our friendship will suffer."

Gabriel could see the tears in her eyes. On the one hand, he wanted to tell her how he felt. He wanted to tell her that she was the reason the sun rose, the reason it set, and the reason he battled demons. On the other hand, he wanted to let her sleep. He knew the toll the spells and the enchanted world took on her mind.

"There isn't anything you could say for me to run away. It's been on my mind for a while now, and I'm sorry I just couldn't hide it any longer. We never know what will happen in life with the demons of the past, the evil trolls, and whatever other ugly evil decides to rear it's head next week. I will save the rest for another day. For now, just know you are my everything, too," said Gabriel.

Magdalena gave Gabriel the biggest bear hug she could muster. He opened her front door, she stepped inside while saying good night and locked the front door. He turned and walked through the little white picket fence gate.

Smiling ear to ear, he had the answer to the one question he needed to be answered tonight. She had feelings for him, the same that he had for her. They were young with plenty of time to see where it went, but secretly he hoped Magdalena would one day be his girlfriend. Although she would always be busy battling demons or some kind of evil, he would always be right there by her side.

With that last thought, Gabriel skipped all the way home under the light of the full moon.

~ The end ~

~ Author News ~

M. Gail Grant would like to thank her readers and would kindly ask you to leave a review on GoodReads and the vendor from which you purchased your book if you feel inclined to do so! She is very grateful for your feedback and thoughts for future readers.

Join our mailing list to receive periodic updates on new releases, sale information, and local author events:

MGailGrant.com
Facebook.com/MGailGrant
Twitter.com/MGailGrant
Instagram.com/MGailGrant

~ Other Reads ~

by

M. Gail Grant:

Magdalena Gottschalk:
The Crooked Trail

Magdalena Gottschalk:
The Slippery Slope

... Coming Soon ...

Magdalena Gottschalk:
The Grand Ball

Made in the USA
Columbia, SC
28 November 2021

49798947R00124